Praise for Agustina Bazterrica and

# TENDER IS THE FLESH

*

Winner of the 2017 Clarín Novela Prize,
First Prize in the 2004/2005 City of Buenos Aires Awards
for Unpublished Stories,
and First Prize in the 2009 Edmundo Valadés Awards
for the Latin American Short Story

*

"From the first words of the Argentine novelist Agustina Bazterrica's second novel, *Tender Is the Flesh*, the reader is already the livestock in the line, reeling, primordially aware that this book is a butcher's block, and nothing that happens next is going to be pretty."

—*The New York Times Book Review*

"The novel is horrific, yes, but fascinatingly provocative (and Orwellian) in the way it exposes the lengths society will go to deform language and avoid moral truths."

—Taylor Antrim, *Vogue*

"Taut and thought-provoking . . . a chilling and alarmingly prophetic book . . . timely, crucial."

—*Words Without Borders*

"Propulsive and deranged . . . a book that will stick with you for a long time."

—Thrillist

"A sagacious and calculated exploration of the limits of moral ambiguity; it sears and devastates."

—Booklist (starred review)

"A page-turner . . . An unrelentingly dark and disquieting look at the way societies conform to committing atrocities."

—Kirkus Reviews

"This book will pull you in, take hold, and not let go until you reach the final page—perhaps far longer than that. Without a doubt, my favorite read of this year."

—Christina Dalcher, author of Vox

"What a compelling, terrible beauty this novel is. My heart was breaking even as my skin was crawling."

—Lisa McInerney, author of The Glorious Heresies

"Provocative, muscular, and entirely unforgiving, this terrifying novel is a timely reminder that words have the power to strip us of our humanity. I gulped it down with my heart racing."

—Sue Rainsford, author of Follow Me to Ground

"A brutal tale of what humans are capable of inflicting on themselves when social norms collapse. Grotesque, gloriously nasty. Utterly compelling."

—Lucie McKnight Hardy, author of Water Shall Refuse Them

"A skin-crawling yet compelling read."

—*Refinery29*

"Grimly engrossing with a sucker-punch ending."

—*The Times* (UK)

"This is a hideous, bold, and unforgettable vision of the future. Just make sure you've eaten before picking it up."

—*i-D* (UK)

"[A] thrilling dystopia that everyone should read for Bazterrica's stunning, electrifying language and storytelling—that is, if you can stomach it."

—*Dazed* (UK)

"Horribly effective . . . This provocative novel expertly wields a double-edged cleaver . . ."

—*The Guardian* (UK)

"A compelling dystopian novel."

—*The Independent* (UK)

"Told with a chilly aloofness that makes the horror of it all the more disturbing."

—*Financial Times* (UK)

"Sitting comfortably? Not after even the tiniest nibble of this gut-churning, brilliantly realized novel."

—*Daily Mail* (UK)

"Unflinching . . . engaging."

—*SFX* (UK)

"At what price is a world without animals viable? That's the question posted by Argentine author Agustina Bazterrica. . . . With an artfulness perfectly calibrated with irony, [she] presents an astounding portrait of a humanity ready to do anything to satisfy itself, even at its own expense.

—*Le Monde* (France)

"A dystopic fable as chilling as it is compelling."

—*Paris Match* (France)

"Hypnotic . . . [Bazterrica's] hell is akin to that of Richard Fleischer's and *Soylent Green.*"

—*L'Obs* (France)

"From a fear of the future (overpopulation and a shortage of meat), Bazterrica has penned a stunning novel on the plasticity of our moral values, and what Hannah Arendt called 'the banality of evil.'"

—*Lire*

"Heiress to Orwell, the Argentine author deploys a voice as vivid as it is chilling. In an increasingly dehumanized world, she pushes us to a dizzying reflection on violence, love, [and] power."

—*Livres Hebdo*

"This Argentine novel, winner of the Clarín prize in 2017, pulls no punches. Agustina Bazterrica succeeds in normalizing a cruelty beyond words."

—*Le Canard Enchaîné*

"A political fable, a denunciation by way of absurdity on the fate society reserves for animals and a love story outside conventional norms, [this novel] seizes you and won't let go.

—*Télérama*

"Skilled seamstress, Agustina [Bazterrica] unspools her thread and stitches the words to bring us wherever she wants, upending our sensibility through a ride that has everything in a final twist."

—*Maze*

"A fable on the gruesome side of the modern world, impressionistic and poetic."

—*Clarín*

"A biting and uncompromising expression of what happens daily in our society."

—*La Nacion*

"Hypnotic, gruesome, beautiful, captivates the reader within moments."

—El Imparcial

"Heavy, magnetic, disturbing—the novel of the year."

—*Culturamas*

# NINETEEN CLAWS AND A BLACK BIRD

*stories*

## AGUSTINA BAZTERRICA

*translated from the Spanish by*
**SARAH MOSES**

**SCRIBNER**

NEW YORK   LONDON   TORONTO   SYDNEY   NEW DELHI

Scribner

An Imprint of Simon & Schuster, Inc.

1230 Avenue of the Americas

New York, NY 10020

Copyright © 2020 by Agustina Bazterrica

English language translation copyright © 2023 by Sarah Moses

Previously published in Great Britain in 2023 by Pushkin Press
Originally published in Argentina in 2020
by Alfaguara as *Diecinueve garras y un pájaro oscuro*

First Scribner trade paperback edition June 2023

SCRIBNER and design are registered trademarks of The Gale Group, Inc., used under license by Simon & Schuster, Inc., the publisher of this work.

For information about special discounts for bulk purchases, please contact Simon & Schuster Special Sales at 1-866-506-1949 or business@simonandschuster.com.

The Simon & Schuster Speakers Bureau can bring authors to your live event. For more information or to book an event, contact the Simon & Schuster Speakers Bureau at 1-866-248-3049 or visit our website at www.simonspeakers.com.

Interior design by Kyle Kabel

Manufactured in the United States of America

3   5   7   9   10   8   6   4

Library of Congress Cataloging-in-Publication Data has been applied for.

ISBN 978-1-6680-1266-6
ISBN 978-1-6680-1267-3 (ebook)

*To my grandmother, my mother, and my sister:*
*my heroines.*

*To Liliana Díaz Mindurry,*
*for all that you've taught me and more.*

# CONTENTS

A Light, Swift, and Monstrous Sound     1

Roberto     9

Unamuno's Boxes     13

Candy Pink     19

Anita and Happiness     33

Dishwasher     39

Earth     59

Perfect Symmetry     67

The Wolf's Breath     75

Teicher vs. Nietzsche     77

The Dead     85

# CONTENTS

Elena-Marie Sandoz     91

The Slowness of Pleasure     99

No Tears     103

The Continuous Equality of the Circumference     113

A Hole Hides a House     119

Hell     125

Architecture     129

Mary Carminum     133

The Solitary Ones     147

. . . the somber bird perched on my chest
dining on my tongue.

—Elena Anníbali

Haven't you ever / wondered what it would be like
if instead of hands you had claws / or roots or fins,
what it would be like / if the only way to live were
in silence / or emitting murmurs or shouts /
of pleasure or pain or fear, if there were no
words / and the soul of every living thing were
measured / by the intensity of what it
once was capable of / and released?

—Claudia Masin

# NINETEEN CLAWS
## AND A
## BLACK BIRD

# A LIGHT, SWIFT, AND MONSTROUS SOUND

First the dentures fell onto the blue tiles of your patio. They broke in two, and it was that harsh, metallic sound that stopped you in your tracks. You crouched down to pick up one of the halves. It was clearly old and belonged to an unkempt person, someone with no dental hygiene whatsoever. You wondered who this could be, whether it was some neighbor who'd dropped them or thought to throw them onto your patio. You were about to take one more step, to pick up the other half, but you stood there thinking it was a little ironic that dentures had fallen precisely onto your patio, a dentist's patio, and it was at that moment that Menéndez's body fell, seconds after his dentures.

The sound of Menéndez's body plummeting, breaking, dying on the blue tiles of your patio, that vulgar and profound noise, paralyzed you. You clutched the dentures until they cut your hand as you watched Menéndez's blood stain your patio. You thought you could hear his blood dirtying your tiles; you thought you understood the sound to be like the cold, a cold that's light, swift, and monstrous.

You crouched down as though by force of habit and picked up the other piece, which was very close to your bare foot, your shoeless foot, a January 1 foot, at home on holiday, at the start of a new year that would be productive and happy, while your neighbor Menéndez lay dead on the blue tiles of your patio.

You looked at Menéndez's body, which was naked and had no dentures. You smiled because it would have been very easy for you to fix his dentures and you would have done so free of charge, because Menéndez was your neighbor, had been your neighbor. His mouth was now open, empty. The expression on his face was one of hatred, a hatred that was pure, specific, directed, a hatred targeted at the woman who lived on the ground floor in apartment B, at you.

You saw Menéndez's red blood, which was essentially black, move slowly toward your right foot, and you became aware that half a centimeter had prevented you from ending up underneath the frail but forceful bones, the yellowed and oily, murderous skin, the toothless mouth of the filthy old man that was Menéndez.

The sound of his body committing suicide on the blue tiles of your patio, that sound, which now seemed faint, almost insignificant, but that had been excessive, cruel, had become mixed up with the question of why he'd gone and killed himself on your patio. He'd had several others, abandoned patios, larger patios, flower-filled patios, empty patios, beautiful patios, patios with no neighbor hanging clothes barefoot in a nightgown on January 1. You looked up and understood that the only way Menéndez could have killed himself on your patio was by climbing onto the wall of his rooftop terrace. Menéndez had chosen your patio; he'd chosen you. He'd tried to kill you, or at the very least, harm you. Menéndez had gone to so much effort, you thought, and yet had been so ineffective.

You shuddered when you saw the blood run slowly, but ferociously, around the edges of your foot. The soft sound of the red liquid moving almost in silence made your body go cold and you wanted to scream, but all you did was stare at the dentures.

You heard the neighbors behind the door to your apartment. So many neighbors, so many patios, so much noise. They rang the bell, knocked, called out your name, but you were looking, mesmerized, at Menéndez's horribly made dentures, and you laughed, because you understood that this was an awful joke fate had played on you, one of those stories that happen only to a colleague's cousin's friend's girlfriend, who tells it in a way that's humorous and not very convincing at some forgotten gathering, mixing your story, your truth, with improbable urban legends, while everyone laughs and drinks and thinks that a neighbor will never fall on their heads. And you felt that people like you didn't deserve this, courteous people, professional people, people with their lives together and in order, people you considered to be good, because you were an exemplary person, your values were in the right place, and you were destined for success. That Menéndez's repugnant, naked body was an omen at the start of your year, a sign from the heavens, was simply unacceptable. That an everyday appliance, an object of decidedly little value, such as used dentures, had intervened and saved your young and vital body, your perfect and radiant teeth, from ending up under Menéndez's decaying bones, his aging, sweating skin, was an insult.

You remained there, crouched down and clutching the dentures, the two halves in your hand, while someone knocked your door in and the neighbors and police entered, yelling things and crying out, their sentences full of panic, and you heard odd words like *señorita, how awful, suicide, neighbor, ambulance, male, shock, police station, poor girl, file a report, what a tragedy, Menéndez, we're nothing.*

Someone put a blanket over your shoulders, though it was the middle of summer, and human stupidity seemed so natural to you, the automatic and senseless gesture to protect. Someone tried to move you, to sit you down on a chair, but you didn't want the edges of your foot to lose contact with the bestial yet almost inaudible sound of the blood; you didn't want to stop hearing it. They brought you a chair and you sat down, your bare feet red and soaked.

Your fourth-floor neighbor came over. You recognized her by the stench of confinement and ten-cent incense. She put her hand over her mouth and said, How dreadful, my dear, how dreadful, what a tragedy, God save us, how awful. She touched your hair and you moved her hand away as if you were ridding yourself of a plague, a venereal infection, a biblical curse. She huffed, indignant, and said something like, The nerve, and, Rude young lady, but she said it all together, Thenerveofthisrudeyounglady. You asked yourself if there was a wise woman out there who could teach you to behave in a civilized manner next to your neighbor's naked, dentureless body. She left for the kitchen, taking with her the smell of mothballs and breath saturated with a mix of rancid medication and alcohol masked with coffee. You didn't care that the other women from the building joined the one from the fourth floor, and that all of these shocked neighbors made remarks, talked, breathed, while they pointed at Osvaldito, which is what they called Menéndez, whom they'd apparently known for such a long time. You thought that the older women who gathered in the hallways with their short, poorly dyed hair, their long, painted nails, and small, amputated brains, were united by a common misguided imbecility. They shared an excessive passion for tiny, hyperkinetic dogs, controversial breeds that in general tend to be programmed with minute but shrill yelps. These women come across as completely inoffensive beings, but they live comfortably submerged in a combination of evil and normalcy produced by an unhealthy amount of leisure time, the impunity of old age, the need to be present for every occurrence that involves someone else in order to talk about it later in the hallways, in the elevator, during building meetings, at the bakery, at the front door, with the superintendent, with the neighbors in other buildings, with those among them who were fortunate enough not to have been in that rude young lady's place.

You looked at them closely and they seemed to you a despicable group of humans. This group had settled into your kitchen, was helping itself to water from the fridge and smoking impertinently, which you found more violent than the sound of Menéndez exploding on your patio. Human evil knows no limits, you said. You repeated this sentence, your foot bloody, and thought that you led an ordinary life in which you were happy fixing other people's ailing teeth and mouths, in which you felt protected cleaning the suction cannula, or a certain power while you held the #15 blade scalpel, or the spirit of adventure when you looked for rebellious cavities, or important when you gave threatening and serious talks on oral hygiene. And on occasion, on a January 1, something simple could happen, like a neighbor falling onto your patio, and all the talks and all the apparent security of your home would be reduced to an interminable string of platitudes, and to get away from them, you would consider it preferable to listen to the opaque silence of the blood touching your right foot.

You lift your gaze from your foot (from that bizarre foot), and from the blood (from that unfamiliar blood). Two people take notes and pictures of the dead neighbor whose body is on your patio. You look at Menéndez as though you're seeing him for the first time, and you understand that the sound of the naked, toothless body belonging to the filthy old man that he was, the sound of him breaking on the blue tiles of your patio, encased you in anarchy, in the chaos originating in the neighbors who look at you with feigned pity and a certain cordial disdain, in the police who talk to you with words that are imperative, broken, mechanical, in the world that's oppressively civilized and atrocious.

You cover yourself a little more with the blanket, though it's a hot day, because now you know, with an acute certainty, that the sound forced you out of your ordered happiness, shattered your little life of comfort, wise choices, and adequate truths. There it is, the blow that was minuscule and forceful, the explosion of Menéndez's body inside yours, under your bones. It's a faint feeling, but you intuit that it's definitive, irreversible. You inhale and exhale and the merciless sound invades the hollows of your home, the city, the world. It's like the water in an underground river you can't see; it's hidden behind the blood, lurking, but you hear it wounding, with a relentless, light, and monstrous silence, the inside of your thoughts in the center of your cerebral cortex.

# ROBERTO

I have a bunny between my legs. A black one. My bunny's name is Roberto, but it could have been Ignacio or even Carla. I call him Roberto because he's shaped like a Roberto. He's cute because he's hairy and sleeps a lot. I told my friend Isabel. I said, "Isa, the other day a bunny grew between my legs. Do you have one too?" We went to the bathroom at school and she took off her underwear. There was nothing there. She asked me to show her Roberto, but I was embarrassed and I said no. Isabel got mad and said that she'd shown me between her legs and that I was a dummy and she didn't believe me at all. She's a dummy too.

Yesterday Isabel told our math teacher what I'd said about Roberto. Mr. García laughed and called me over to talk to him. "Is what your friend Isabel tells me true?"

"No."

"It is true, I saw it!" the dummy yelled. "Mamá told me that nobody has a bunny between their legs, but she has a black bunny! I saw it, teacher!"

I told her she was a liar because I hadn't shown her anything. I yelled that she was a dummy and a liar and that I didn't want to be her friend anymore. Isabel started to cry. I didn't feel bad because now she's not my friend. Mr. García laughed. He told Isabel to go home and said that later he would explain some things to her. Then he sat down next to me and said, "You're very pretty. Isabel doesn't know anything, don't pay attention to her." He kissed me and then he did it again. He told me that after class tomorrow he wanted to see my little bunny. He wanted to see it so he could teach it to be on its best behavior.

I waited for him. He told me to follow him to the bathroom because nobody was supposed to find out about our secret.

"What's your bunny's name?"

"Roberto."

"What a strange name for a bunny! Can I see him?"

"I'm embarrassed."

He sat down next to me and kissed me a lot. He told me I was his favorite student and that I was the prettiest one. "Show him to me, be a good girl. I won't tell anyone." He talked a lot and looked at me, and he didn't talk like he does when he's in class, because he looked at me loads and then he took my hands and told me to lift up my skirt. "Show me your little bunny, Roberto," he said, but I told him Roberto doesn't like to be called little because he's big now and a grown-up. Mr. García took off my underwear while he kissed my face and hair and mouth and told me to be a good little girl because he was going to teach me a lot of things. When he saw Roberto, he went still and opened his mouth. He was so still that I thought he was playing the statues game. Roberto moved his ears and bared his teeth. Mr. García screamed and ran away. Roberto went back to sleep.

# UNAMUNO'S BOXES

get in the taxi at 900 Alem Avenue. I throw my purse and bag of clothes, the folder with my notes, and the envelope with the receipts on the seat. While I look for my gloves, I say, To Flores, the corner of Bilbao and Membrillar. Dumb name, Membrillar, frivolous. I imagine a hero addicted to cans of membrillo jam. Should I take Rivadavia or Independencia? I can't find my gloves and am slow to answer. It doesn't matter, take whatever you like. Independencia will get us there faster, señora. Señora? Did he just call me señora? I find the gloves, calm myself down, don't answer. Señora, I'll take Independencia, then. I still don't answer.

I look around the taxi. An ashtray that's empty, clean; a sign saying "Pay with Change" without the please or the thank you; a pink pacifier hanging from the rearview mirror; a dog with no dignity wagging its head, saying yes to everything, to everyone. The aura of static cleanliness, of calculated orderliness, exasperates me. I take off my gloves, look for my keys, put them in my coat pocket. Old age that's covered up irritates me. I look out the window. I'm drowsy.

Do you mind if I put some music on, sweetheart? I look at the driver, disconcerted. When exactly did I go from señora to sweetheart? Was it the magnitude of 9 de Julio Avenue that led his brain to make faulty connections? Was it my pseudo-interest in his natural habitat that led him to abandon formality? I don't mind, I answer. He puts cumbia on, and I do mind. I look at the driver's information so I know the exact name to curse in my head. Pablo Unamuno. The irony surprises me. I never would have taken the bearer of so distinguished a last name for a cumbia enthusiast. I laugh at my idiotic elitism, then uncross my legs in an attempt to cover this up. I look at his photo. Either it was taken recently or Señor Unamuno uses the same formula for immortality on himself as he does on his car. It's cold, but I imagine his shirt is open so it's crystal clear he exercises, lifts weights, bags of cement, bags of receipts, notes, clothes, literary and philosophical theories. He stops at a light, glances at me in the mirror, smiles. He places his arm behind the passenger seat, and, hanging from his wrist, I see a gold bracelet with AMANDA on it. I suspect she's the owner of the pacifier. If she was the mother of the owner of the pacifier, the bracelet would be hidden. Straight hair, ripped jeans, he's confident this look is enough. I cross my legs. I'm bored by beauty that's easy, saturated.

Then I see them. The lights from Juan Bautista Alberdi Avenue reflect off his nails—nails cut with the dedication granted only to the most valuable things. Unamuno's arm is still resting on the passenger seat and I can directly examine the two layers of transparent nail polish applied with the patience of the obsessive, with the precision of the enlightened. We stop suddenly at another light and I move forward a little, confirming that his cuticles are impeccable. I feel a rush and open the window. What would Juan Bautista Alberdi have thought of all this? He wouldn't have been able to understand that true genius is concentrated in mundane, banal details, not in treatises on diplomacy or erudite literature. He wouldn't have caught the importance of the insignificant. I settle into the seat and close the window. The cold distracts me.

I think: Unamuno is concealing something with his nails. Their perfection can have been conceived only by a mind that's distinct, superior. A mind capable of crossing limits, of exploring new dimensions. I reckon: Unamuno's secret is hidden in a space that's familiar, quotidian. He requires constant contact with his object of pleasure. I surmise: the taxi is his inner world. He alone has unlimited access. It provides him with the privacy and daily interaction he requires. Where could his secrets be? Under the seat? No, too complicated. In the glove compartment? Yes. It's the perfect spot for secrets. Behind the car manual, he keeps clippers, nail polish, cotton, and two boxes that are transparent, impeccable. In one, he collects his nails as an example of the sublime. In the other, the perfectible nails of his victims. Yes, Señor Juan Bautista, Unamuno is a serial killer.

I unbutton my coat. I elaborate: He's not just any serial killer, one who's numerical, expansive, inclusive, ordinary. Don't pay Unamuno the attention he's due, and he'll pass for a person with no great aspirations. Of course, you need to know how to look, because he leads a life that's consistent, if alarming. He's patient. Selective. Ascetic. He's dangerous. The pacifier is a planned diversion for those who don't know, for those who don't want to know. The docile dog is a false manifestation of an existence that's trivial, resigned. I infer that the AMANDA bracelet belonged to his first victim. A woman who looked dejected, but young. Disoriented and alone. Unable to resist; therefore, easy. Her long nails red and unkempt.

Unamuno didn't settle for immediate gratification. He didn't rape her in the taxi and throw her into a ditch. No. He carried out a ritual.

Without knowing how it happened, Amanda found that she was naked. She couldn't move, or talk, but she was completely conscious. Unamuno bathed her in jasmine water, wrapped her in a towel to dry her off, put a clean dress on her, made her up, dried her hair very slowly, combing it with his fingers, perfumed her, left her on the bed, and took off his clothes. But before this, he allowed an unexpected cello to envelop them in the merciless serenity of Bach's Suite No. 1

in G Major. Naked, he filed her nails, caressed them, cut her cuticles, removed the polish, cleaned them with warm water, kissed them, applied a strengthening coat, put mint-scented lotion on them, massaged it into her hands, placed them on a clean towel, and painted her nails with two layers of red polish. When he was finished, he rested her hands on his naked body, waiting for the polish to dry. Throughout the process, from within her immobility, Amanda understood she was going to die a strange and useless death. Still, she couldn't avoid feeling that it was right, because it was careful, pleasant, thorough, gentle. Unamuno made sure she felt a serene freedom, a sharp freshness. After she died, he cut her nails with a dedication bordering on devotion and put them in one of the transparent boxes.

Excuse me, sweetheart, can you tell me where to turn onto Bilbao? I settle back into the seat, open the window, button up my coat, and tell him. I cross my legs. Breathe. Try to calm myself down. I look out the window to stop thinking, but I can't. I look at my nails. They're long, unkempt. I think about Amanda and ask, Is that your daughter's pacifier? Unamuno coughs, turns off the radio, looks surprised. We stop at a light and he avoids my question by crouching down and opening the glove compartment. I lean forward and all I see are papers and rags. I feel like an idiot. I want to yank the head off the disciplined dog, the dog incapable of saying no. I put my gloves on angrily. I curse the cumbia, the nails, the taxi, and Unamuno's awful simplicity.

How much do I owe you? One eighty-four. I decide to pay with exact change, to punish him for his healthy mind, his lawful life, his clean hands. I gather my bags, grab my keys, open the door. What I want is for him to wait, to exercise the serial killer patience he never developed. I take off my gloves and put them in my purse. I look for my wallet, take out the change, and count it. I take out the bills, count them. As I hand him the money, a coin falls into the space between the two front seats, a space that I realize also contains a box with a lid. Unamuno takes off the lid to look for the coin. He takes it off fully and he takes it off slowly. He looks at me. Smiles. For a second I freeze. Then I'm able to breathe, and I lean forward to see clippers, nail polish, cotton, and two transparent boxes. Suddenly, I close the taxi door, grab his arm, move closer, and say: Let's go, Unamuno. Take me with you, you know where.

# CANDY PINK

*— For my sister, Pili, and for my girlfriends —*

After you there's nothing,
there's nothing left, nothing at all.

—Alejandro Lerner

<u>*Step ONE*</u>

Observe the tears falling on your fingers. Think of diamonds. Picture Elizabeth Taylor. Long for violet eyes and successive husbands. Mistake. Backtrack. You don't need more men in your life. You want to crash Penelope Pitstop's car. Look for a sheet of paper and a pencil. Write the word "list" and enumerate the items you need to purchase in order to die with the style and dignity of a cartoon character.

LIST:

1. Tracksuit, an elegant one, designed for a sculpted physique.

*Ignore last detail, about the sculpted physique. Proceed, unfazed.*

2. White pinup sunglasses
3. Parasol with bow
4. White go-go boots
5. ACME brand car with prominent lips and eyes serving as a hood

Don't explore the disturbing fact that you want to die in a car with a human face.

Remember there is no money in your bank account. Tear the sheet of paper and throw the pencil into the fish tank. Watch your fish look at you with its deformed eyes. Assume your fish is a freak of nature and fail to comprehend the reason you purchased it. Attempt to analyze why you gave a fish that's permanently unaware of you the name Pepino. Ponder the specific motive for giving the fish you call "cucumber" loving nicknames such as "many-colored Pepino" or "my Pepinito," as though it were possible to hug this fish, to transmit affection to it through the water. Acknowledge that a fish is not a vegetable and that your fish is a single color:

a discolored yellow, a repugnant yellow. Observe the castle made of purple plastic in which the pencil landed. Reflect on the fundamental purpose of a fish having, as its apparent dwelling, a castle that it exceeds in size. Discover that an answer to such a question does not exist.

Concentrate on the word *purpose*. Consider the following question objectively: What is the purpose of love? Feel depressed because you don't have an answer. Open the bag of Kellogg's potato chips and munch on them compulsively. Experience a void caused by the lack of structure and certainty when it comes to love in the universe. Pick up the vase with brilliantly colored Chinese dragons on it. Launch it at the center of Van Gogh's *Sunflowers*. Find that you're sick of Mona Lisa's smile; she's looking at you from the wall where the glass covering *Sunflowers* shattered into pieces. Rejoice at not being Mona Lisa. Think that there is something vaguely animal about that face. Philosophize: "Is it because of the unconscious association I'm making with the word for monkey, *mona*, or because I find that woman to be frankly disagreeable?" Remember that he insisted on buying those prints. Take a red permanent marker and draw fangs on Mona Lisa's smile. Cite Duchamp and draw her a mustache. Laugh. Loudly. Don't question who Duchamp was or why he once drew a mustache on a sacred icon of art. You don't have time to delve into stylistic mysteries, not when you're in the middle of an emotional crisis. Detest *Sunflowers*. Become aware of the profound antipathy you have always felt for these paintings. Finish this sentence by adding: "Cheap paintings." Picture the hatred. Let it flow. Throw Mona Lisa out the window. Observe Mona Lisa and her mustache plummet onto an abandoned rooftop. Next toss *Sunflowers* out and see it fly, without the weight of the glass, through the city's power lines. Feel a secret pleasure, but don't acknowledge it, because you're going through a period of grief and rage. Perceive a man looking at you sadly, while he leans against a parked car.

Associate the car with a key factor, which is that he'd promised to teach you how to drive, but never did. Call him a coward and whisper the words *fucking coward*. Surprise yourself with your audacity. You never curse. His cowardice is far superior to the curse's intensity; as such, yell: "FUCKING COWARD." Break the words up with significant pauses: "Fuck Ing Cow Ard." Burst into weepy syllables: "Fuck, Fuck, Fuuuck, Fuck, Ahhh, Ing, Ing, Iiiing, Cow, Cow, Cooow, Ahhh, Aaaaard."

Examine the collateral damage caused by the intensification of your crazed emotions. Consider that you have only attained part of your objective.

### Step *TWO*

Look for the Kleenex box. Become aware of Disney's princesses looking at you from the cardboard. Long to turn into Snow White, then Cinderella, then Sleeping Beauty. Demand that fate allow you uninterrupted sleep in a crystal bed and suggest the detail about beauty can be overlooked. You want to sleep and to dream you're with him for always, eating partridges. You're vegetarian, but don't pay attention to this detail. Forget that meat disgusts you and eat the partridges because this is the guarantee of happiness. Think this through: "Is my desire to be with him forevermore a utopia?" Relate the word *utopia* to the word *revolution*. Recall the Che Guevara T-shirt he had on when he met you. Think about Cuba and cry for the revolutions that materialized and those that never did. Dirty a dozen Kleenexes and scatter them on the floor. Sit down next to the phone and look at it in such a way that your eyes hurt. Check that it works. Listen to the answering machine and when a voice announces, "You have no new messages," repress the imperious need to butcher the person, or the machine, who recorded this sentence in an impersonal tone, one that nevertheless places a slight stress on the word *no*, thus emphasizing, in a subversive manner, the fact that no one ever calls you.

Look with surprise at the notepad he gave you on your one-month anniversary. The notepad has a water transfer print of Dalí's *The Persistence of Memory* on it. Acknowledge that you find the metaphor of time melting to be a banality repeated ad nauseam, but permit yourself to feel a certain attachment to the image because it was a gift from him.

Call him. Hang up.

Become flustered when you hear the phone ring. Control the justified need to jump for joy. Hold your breath, and when you answer, shaking, feel a reef knot in your stomach. Say:

"Hhhhello." Warning: The tone you should use is that of veiled suffering. Listen to an operator offer you a plan to speak to your loved one free of charge. Note the reef knot transforming into a cluster of poisonous spiders that crawl along your throat. Shout: "I DON'T HAVE A LOVED ONE." Hang up. The spiders are now scorpions.

*     *     *

*Exercise*: Memorize the moments of happiness over the course of your life and note them down on a piece of paper under the title "Happy List."

*Objective*: Strengthen your inner confidence.

HAPPY LIST:

- The day I met him
- The day he kissed me for the first time
- The day of our one-month anniversary
- The day he gave me a flower
- The day he moved in with me
- The day he gave me a star
- The day he told me I would always be his love

*Conclusion of exercise*: Eat Media Hora candies. Make yourself sick and want to spit them out, but don't because they were his favorite candies. Recognize this as a sincere and passionate way to honor him.

*       *       *

Call him a second time. When the answering machine picks up, hang up. Disappointed, call his phone to hear the message you recorded together, when you were happy: "Hi, leave us a message after the tone. Beeeeeeeepppppp, hahhhhaaahhhaaaha." Imagine his chest being opened and a bomb being placed inside it. Commemorate Hiroshima. Feel Judeo-Christian guilt for the dead you never knew. Experience oedipal guilt for the evil in the world, for war in particular, for death in general. Regret that you're unable to poke your eyes out, that you don't have the courage, that you don't know how to live through a real tragedy, that you're not Greek. Recall the movie *Hiroshima mon amour*. Hate the word *amour*, hate the French language. Yell: "I HATE PARIS, I HATE LOVE." Remember that he wanted to propose to you at the Eiffel Tower. Explore this concept. Deduce that not only was it an unfeasible plan, it was an unpardonable lie and you believed it. Rip apart the poster of the Eiffel Tower stuck above the toilet. Try to understand the secret analogy, the hidden significance, of sticking the Eiffel Tower in this specific location. Know the answer, but ignore it because it's violent, because it's obvious, violently obvious.

Call him a third time. Murmur: "Hi, it's me." Feel like an idiot. Imagine Penelope Pitstop declaring her love to Atom Ant. Remember that he used to call you "hormiguita," his little ant. Yell: "I HATE YOU, PRICK."

Hang up.

Immortalize the moment by throwing the plush lilac phone against the wall with the collection of crystal figurines he gave you in a consecutive, successive manner over the years. Observe the transparent giraffe fly through the air and the translucent pair of lovers sitting on a park bench holding hands fall to the floor. Go over to the figurine of the lovers, pick it up, and verify its status. Intact. Cry. Clutch the figurine and throw it out the window. Contemplate the crystal as it shatters on the asphalt. Confirm that the sad man leaning against the car has not seen you commit a possible assault against an innocent passerby and rejoice at the empty street. Eat Havanna alfajor cookies and sigh, but experience a certain calm on noticing the brilliant glint of the crystal on the asphalt.

Go to the bedroom. Look through the underwear drawer until you find the card he wrote you on your third anniversary. Open the card and read it out loud.

*Beautiful Hormiguita, love of my life:*
*I love you like crazy. I love you more than my life,*
*more than the whole universe.*

*Life without you has no meaning.*
*I love you more than Racing.*

*Your love forevermore.*

Fall limply to the floor. Press the card to your chest and cry effusively. Feel like Grecia Colmenares in the soap opera *María de nadie*, but with the shortcoming of hair that only reaches your shoulders.

When you regain your strength, pick up the phone. Connect it. Verify whether you did indeed succeed at breaking it. Hear the tone and smile with relief.

Take stock of the damage and reach the conclusion that it's not sufficient. The misfortune that overwhelms you weighs far more than a cheap print flying through power lines. Correct yourself and exclaim: "A piece of shit print flying through power lines." Open the window and yell: "SHIT."

<u>*Step THREE*</u>

*Exercise*: Make a collage.

*Objective*: Attain emotional well-being.

Look for the photos in which you appear with him.

Throw them on the floor.

Organize them according to whether you felt a greater or lesser degree of happiness at the time.

Sit down on the shaggy carpet, which imitates a tiger that has died in a nonexistent hunt. Remember that he was going to teach you to hunt, but when you told him you were not interested in killing innocent animals, he gave you a revolver and the carpet.

Take a close look at your collage on the brown tiles and experience pain poisoned by the spiders and scorpions. Pity yourself and announce: "This collage depicts my one and only love." Give yourself sufficient time to repeat the sentence again and again until the words lose all meaning.

Light a cigarette. Cough. You don't smoke, but the cigarettes are the Marlboro Lights he forgot after packing his bags. While you take the cigarette and burn out his eyes in each of the photos where he looks beautiful and is hugging you, whisper: "You broke my heart into a thousand pieces." Sway back and forth and assume that you have entered a state from which there is no return. Wish to become a serial killer, but know that you don't have the necessary lucidity to commit an assassination, or two, or three, or twenty.

Lie down on the carpet and smoke, brooding.

Rip the photos and put them under the garden gnome on your balcony. Look at the gnome's face and find you're surprised by the disturbing likeness he bears to your fish. Change your mind. Stick the photos in the microwave and select the maximum time and highest temperature. Situate Enrique (the gnome) in the fish tank. Don't concern yourself further with his fate, nor that of Pepino, or the microwave.

*Conclusion of exercise*: Take charge of the present moment, eat Don Satur biscuits and look into the void.

\*         \*         \*

### Step FOUR

Think about television personality Susana Giménez. Ask yourself what Susana Giménez has to do with everything that's happening to you. Feel your sanity dissolve in an animal print. Notice the jaguar, zebra, and Dalmatian spots and stripes cast a shadow over all reason.

Note the presence, on top of the television, of the Chinese lucky cat he bought you when you went out for mixed chow fan at Todos Contentos, the restaurant in Chinatown. Have the certainty that this cat is the cause of all your misfortune, because on the next day, he left you. Go to the kitchen, fill a pot with water, turn the heat up to maximum, and introduce the cat. Let it boil.

Run to the bathroom and look at yourself in the mirror. Confirm that you're pale and haggard. Recognize that you're no longer Grecia Colmenares and have transformed into the

Andrea del Boca from the soap opera *Celeste*, not the one from
*Perla negra*. Sigh with conviction and assert: "I'm not crazy."
Accept that this is a lie, look for the pearly red nail polish, and
write on the glass: "I love you, my wretched and beautiful dog."

Experience a feeling of ecstasy, run to the phone, and call
him for the fourth time. Hear a woman's voice answer. Hang
up and say to yourself: "Wrong number." Call him for the
fifth time and, when you hear the woman's voice, find you're
unable to speak. Witness that before answering, he says to
the woman's voice: "Leave it, my love, give me the phone,
hormiguita of mine."

Hang up slowly, and as you do, know with absolute certainty what the next step is going to be.

## *Step FIVE*

Go up to the window and gauge the distance between the
asphalt and your body. Intuit that there exists a possibility of
ending up badly hurt but alive. Laugh. Halfheartedly. Munch
on Amor cookies in an automatic fashion. Notice the brutal
irony of fate—you're eating a brand of cookies called "Love"—
and throw the bag in the trash.

Go to the closet and open all the boxes of shoes. Feel
an exultant energy when you find a bag of clothes he never
picked up. Throw it in the washing machine and add bleach.
Cut the tiger's head off and put it in the oven. Put the oven

on maximum. Continue to look among the shoes and find the firearm he gave you. Examine it carefully. Confirm it's loaded. Remember that you once heard the television personality Mirtha Legrand say that women don't shoot themselves. "Women," said Mirtha on her lunch program, "poison themselves or take pills because it's less bloody and because before they die they take into account those who will still be alive and have to clean up." Reject this thought for being old-fashioned, but admire Señora Legrand's general knowledge. Delight in the undeniable point that he's the only contact they'll call. After the irreparable damage he caused you, he doesn't deserve the tranquility of a clean death.

Walk slowly to the living room with the love letter in your hand. Look for nails, but remember he took them. Look for Scotch tape, but don't find it. Open the first-aid kit and resort to Band-Aids. Stick the letter on the wall with two Band-Aids, one with Hello Kitty's image on it, the other with Snoopy's.

Feel that you're in the midst of chaos, in the midst of emotional, material, and concrete destruction. Look at the letter and exclaim: "I'm too young to die." Accept the fact that this is an empty statement. Pick up the firearm. Smile with a certain excitement. Place the firearm against your right temple. Allow the feeling that you're doing what's right to flow. Say: "This is what's right." Repeat it. Assert: "This is what's right."

Stop yourself. Breathe and lower the firearm. Contemplate your thoughts. Clear your mind and focus on observing it. Recognize yourself as Mona Lisa, surrounded by crystal giraffes, inside a field of sunflowers, trying to hunt shaggy tigers to deliver to Enrique and the Chinese lucky cat, who are living in the purple castle where plastic watches melt in the flames of the love he and the woman's voice feel, the two of them looking at you and laughing from atop the Eiffel Tower, while Pepino dances with the translucent couple falling out the window right onto the sad man's head, and the man whispers to Penelope Pitstop: "I love you more than Racing." Yell "ENOUGH" and pull the trigger. The instant the bullet perforates your skull, envision a feeling of calm that's pink in color, candy pink.

# ANITA AND HAPPINESS

Pablo detested Anita because he couldn't prove what he'd suspected ever since they'd met: that she was an alien.

He hated her name because it wasn't Ana, plain and simple, Ana with real problems like cellulitis, unpaid bills, or anxiety brought on by the knowledge that human beings are a mere parenthesis between two unknowns. The name Anita evoked a defenseless being, a woman with a fragile constitution and a chronic illness, a woman you'd have to look after just because, for no other reason than that her name bore the diminutive *ita*. But Anita was much more than that, which is why Pablo decided to fall in love with her, if only to confirm whether her apparent weakness could be hiding a mastermind capable of conquering the universe, or a tireless predator harassing the human race.

One of Anita's oddities was her addiction to work. No one could really be a workaholic dependent on cataloging books at the neighborhood library. She'd been hired because of her exceptional memory, and at first Pablo thought she was on the autism spectrum (she was so quiet, rigid, automatic), but when she recited, without pause, the first chapter of a book on supramolecular chemistry, and told him that the discipline was one of her passions, Pablo began to suspect that there was something strange about Anita.

Before she spoke, Anita would close her eyes slowly, as though she were activating some internal device that would dictate her words. She often began her sentences with "I have been thinking," like when she said to Pablo, after closing her eyes, "I have been thinking we ought to engage in sexual intercourse." Pablo looked at her and replied, "So you're saying you want me to fuck you, to really fucking give it to you? Is that what you want, Anita?" He enunciated *Anita* with rage, with disdain, and she closed her eyes, the look on her face that of a civil servant stamping gross-income forms, and answered, "I have been thinking I would." She then stood up and took off her clothes in an orderly fashion, as though she were about to clean a window or throw out expired medication, with a weariness she didn't want Pablo, the human, to notice. Pablo was a little embarrassed to find this turned him on, this ascetic ritual in which she took off her clothes, lay down on the bed, opened her legs, and stared at the ceiling without saying a word.

He believed, more strongly with each passing day, that Anita was on a mission from another planet: "You are going to be called Anita because it sounds sweet, you are going to think with your eyes closed because it looks deep, and you are going to be a workaholic because it seems serious. When you integrate into society, you will collect the largest amount of information possible. That way we can enslave the humans because they are an inferior, defective race. But you will connect to the best specimen you find." It was for this reason that Pablo accepted—with fascination and a bit of contempt—many of Anita's anomalies, like her obsession with letters addressed to the neighbors and with the postman, on whom she spied whenever he came by. Anita removed the letters from the mailbox, read them, and then returned them. Pablo was convinced they were messages in code she had to process, that they were sent by the commanders of Planet X and that the postman was one of her kind, another alien. He also didn't say anything when Anita disappeared for hours or days without notice, because he understood she had to communicate with her fellow aliens and provide them with regular reports on the earthlings' customs.

Anita didn't swear. One day she sliced her finger and said, "The Republic of Argentina cut my finger." Pablo couldn't restrain the urge to laugh out loud, which was followed by the urge to throw her off a cliff. At times like these, he asked himself whether Anita, the supposed intergalactic hunter, was really just an alien who'd been banished from Planet X for being an imbecile.

Pablo loved her, but he couldn't help abhorring her. When he fantasized about grabbing a knife, cutting her in half, and finally finding the extraterrestrial inside her, he would look at her with something resembling admiration and nausea, and she, confused, would close her eyes, and a look of polished cement would come over her face, and she would say, "I have been thinking we need to copulate." With a vague feeling of happiness, Pablo would give himself over to the chaste and artificial ritual, always on the lookout for mechanisms, hidden buttons, hatches that would reveal Anita's body to be nothing more than a vessel that hid the actual extraterrestrial. She didn't seem to mistrust Pablo's exploratory caresses. He believed this was because she was overly focused on remembering the positions, the moans that had to be emitted at the right moments—oh, uh, yes, mmmm, god, a short ah, only with more energy than before—so that Pablo would notice she'd had an orgasm when she was supposed to have one. A tremor never ran through her body, and Pablo was afraid of being a horrible lover to the alien, and of confirming the uselessness of the human species.

Over time, Anita's absences grew more frequent and Pablo began to miss the paranoia he'd felt at her appearing out of nowhere, silently, and looking at him as though he were a stranger, before closing her eyes and saying, "I have been thinking we need to reproduce," and the mix of hatred and euphoria he felt at her choice of words, because the possibility of their having a hybrid baby filled him with horror and happiness.

One day Anita disappeared completely. Pablo was proud. He felt it meant she'd returned to Planet X with a report of what it was like to live with the human Pablo, an exceptional being. He ignored the neighbors' malicious rumors that Anita had left him for the postman. He looked at them with pity because they existed within their trivial lives and didn't know the truth.

One afternoon, he was on the subway and saw the hexagonal polygon face he'd missed so much. When he went up to her and said, "What are you doing here, Anita?" she answered, "I'm not Anita." Pablo hesitated, but he insisted, "Come on, Anita, don't fuck around, let's go home." She closed her eyes and said, "I'm not Anita, I'm Clarita." Pablo looked at her carefully. She was almost identical to Anita. But there was something different about her eyes, her hair. She was prettier, if an alien could be described in that way. The invasion has begun, Pablo thought, and he felt a mix of terror and joy. He sat down by her side, smiled, and said, "Hi, Clarita, I'm Pablo."

# DISHWASHER

Love drains you, takes with it much of your blood sugar
and water weight. You are like a house slowly losing its
electricity, the fans slowing, the lights dimming and
flickering; the clocks stop and go and stop.

—Lorrie Moore

I

Manhattan had perforated Jane's brain. It had done so simply and brutally. It had perforated it completely. Jane imagined her brain being taken to a sieve factory in secret, at
night. Someone would throw it onto a conveyor belt and the
machines would take charge of the rest. But this wasn't what
most distressed her. That was the light.

"You know," Jane said to Carrie, "it's the solidity of the air,
the light, that I can't bear in New York's streets."

Carrie looked at her, disconcerted, and replied, "The
solidity? What are you talking about, Jane? I don't understand you." Jane sighed, offended by her friend's complacent

naiveté. "Oh, Jane, come on, tell me what you mean. You're always confusing me with your strange, deep sentences."

Jane looked straight at Carrie and smiled. "You wouldn't understand, Carrie, it's just a feeling. The feeling that there are these things that break apart into big pieces that choke me."

"Okay, then, let me tell you something, Jane. That's not possible. It's a product of your tired imagination. You need to see a doctor. Listen, I'm telling you this as a friend, you know that, right? You look exhausted." Jane hated herself for letting the conversation reach this point. She knew what was coming next and lit a cigarette so she wouldn't have to listen to Carrie. "Jeez, Jane, I've told you this so many times. You should go see Dr. Wesselmann. In the last issue of *The New Yorker* he was recommended as one of the best doctors in the city. They gave him five stars. He has impeccable taste in Formica furniture. I saw photos of his Fifth Avenue apartment in the June issue of *Harper's Bazaar*. And he's just dreamy, you know? He's a widower, Jane."

At this, Carrie winked, as she always did, and then looked at Jane silently, in a way that never failed to make her uncomfortable because it seemed as though there were moments when Carrie's brain had no pulse, no beat, when it was totally silent. Jane served her some more lemonade. "You're right, Carrie, I'll go see a doctor." These words put an end to the evening. Carrie gathered her things, stood up, blew Jane some parting kisses from above, turned around, and left.

Jane hated Carrie's air kisses, and having given it some thought, she hated Carrie too, hated everything about her, though she hadn't managed to convey that Carrie wasn't welcome. Jane had tried everything, but Carrie was like a social machine. Her sole function was to go on insignificant visits to insignificant people to make their lives more miserable and insignificant, before making her exit with air kisses. What's more, the ritual was always the same. Carrie rang the bell and entered midway through a sentence, a sentence she'd extracted from some other visit to some other person, as though the time between these visits extended with no apparent pause: ". . . and Mrs. Hamilton laughed and laughed, you know what I'm talking about, of course you do, she was a madwoman laughing like that, wearing that bow with the red spots on her head, it's so horribly out of fashion, and people gave her these disapproving looks, but she kept laughing, she didn't care when the bow slipped off to the side, completely ruining her hair. And she needs to think about her appearance, you know? Because now that she's a divorcée . . ." Carrie went completely silent at this point, her silence full of revulsion at the idea of a person, a woman, having the poor judgment to destroy the sacred artifact that is marriage. Jane knew that Carrie didn't totally spurn her because she was single and there was still hope. Carrie would take responsibility for guiding Jane along the right path of contractual love. ". . . a divorcée, see what I'm saying, Jane? How dare she behave like that?"

All Jane managed to get in was, "Hi, Carrie." She followed her friend to the kitchen, the kitchen in her house, where Carrie was now taking out a shallow dish for the refreshments she'd brought.

". . . and let me tell you something, my husband told me that Mrs. Hamilton has simply lost her mind, did you hear that?"

Jane felt that as well as being a social machine, Carrie was a cowardly machine, because whenever she had something negative to say about someone, she quoted her husband. Jane imagined him to be an insignificant cog in the social machinery that was Carrie's world. She thought of him as a nut or bolt, seated with a beer, watching the Yankees play the Red Sox, while Carrie talked to him and served refreshments to nobody; as one more piece in the metallic structure that constituted her life. She knew that Carrie's husband would never say things like "Mrs. Hamilton is a madwoman" or "Carrie, your friend Jane looks unfavorable, she lacks a certain spark, do you see what I'm saying? A radiance that certain women possess, those who know what it means to be a woman. Your friend Jane is washed out and that's why she's single." But she did imagine this coming out of Carrie's mechanical mouth. She knew these words had been repeated to all the insignificant individuals to whom Carrie paid her automatic visits. Jane had opted to accept them like she would some other inevitable and tedious aspect of life, as one accepts insects or frozen meat.

Jane wondered whether it might not be a good idea to see Dr. Wesselmann after all. She looked at herself in the mirror and sighed. Her skin was tense. It gave her the appearance of an older woman, a woman who knows that joy and youth are overrated and accepts the consequences of this fact. She lit a cigarette and looked for the ashtray. It was on the table. She stopped, as she always did when she located some object that was unchangeable but seemed alive. No one could be absolutely certain that an oval piece of ceramic wasn't alive. There was always something, a small detail, that gave her cause for doubt. She was horrified by the traces of monstrosity in everyday life. The things that we look at but don't see, whose true essences are unknown to us. The light projected the shadows of the mound of stubbed-out cigarette butts. This detail turned them into entities that Jane was not prepared to accept. She would have liked the cigarettes' cadavers to simply disappear into the air, into the light. But they never did and Jane learned to live with the fear. Then she thought about the sieve that was her brain and wondered whether it was a good idea to smoke. She imagined the smoke escaping through the holes in her head and then transforming into opaque crystals that flew through the air and accumulated, eventually choking her. She laughed at the image, but her mouth was static.

Jane went to the kitchen and opened the fridge. She could unfreeze the beef stew. She wasn't enthusiastic about the idea, but she preferred to eat while watching *I Love Lucy* than to go to the fast-food place where the employees treated her like a stranger. She didn't understand how or why this happened. One of her theories was that because their hormones were running wild, the teenagers who worked there didn't remember the faces of the people they saw almost every day. Jane was also bothered by the pimples on their pink faces; their skin reminded her of pig fat. She knew that the pimples projected an unhealthy shadow. That was why she never looked at the employees directly. They all seemed the same to her: servile copies of themselves. She was unable to tell them apart, even when she tried. But she still went to the fast-food place because she knew, with absolute certainty, that they served the best fries in the city.

She went to the bathroom and looked at herself in the mirror. There were small bruises on her face. She didn't know where they'd come from, and thought that the shadows things projected could have an impact on bodies, leaving marks that nobody could see, except for her, because she recognized the true existential weight of objects. After Jane had this thought, she decided to go see Dr. Wesselmann, not because she felt he could fix the holes in her brain or alleviate the feeling of being damaged, but because she needed her conversations with Carrie to take a turn, she needed to excise these words from her friend's visits: "Jeez, Jane, I've told you this so many times. You should go see Dr. Wesselmann."

II

Jane called Dr. Wesselmann's office to make an appointment. When the secretary asked why she wanted to see the doctor, Jane was only able to say, "It's because of the light."

There was an uncomfortable silence on the other end of the phone and Jane wished she'd thought of a conventional reason like stomach pain or chronic migraines. The secretary said, "So, Mrs. Rosenquist, you're having problems with your vision?"

Jane wanted to respond that that wasn't it, but she said, "Yes, that's correct, that's the problem." She added, "It's Miss, not Mrs.," and agreed on a time for the appointment.

She went to her room and opened the closet. She wanted to look pretty and chose an outfit she wore on special occasions. After all, she was hoping to make a good impression, since Dr. Wesselmann was a widower and she was single. She disliked this thought and blamed Carrie and her damn refreshments and expansive, harmful influence. In a rage, she took the outfit off and stood naked in the middle of the room, unable to react. She looked at herself in the mirror. Her beauty was evanescent. As the years passed, it had transformed into a faint beauty, she no longer saw it as having a presence. She felt insecure about her face because of the small bruises and applied too much makeup to skin that tolerated it less with every passing day. She noticed that a thin layer of foundation had slowly accumulated on her skin. It had a yellowish tone that sometimes appeared gray, but she preferred this to the bruises. The phone rang.

"Hello."

"Jane, it's Sharon."

"Oh, hi, Mother."

"I'm not Mother, Jane, I'm Sharon. How many times do I have to ask you to call me Sharon?"

"Hi, Sharon."

"I'm in Hawaii."

"I know, you called last week."

"Billy is doing lunges on the steps in the pool. I'm in love, Jane, you have got to see him. He's a total dreamboat with his black hair and glistening muscles."

"What happened to Charly?"

"Charly? Who's that?"

"You were in love with Charly last week. You referred to him as the best derrière in this blessed world. Those were your exact words, Mother."

"Oh, right, of course! That's right, Charly. I like Billy better. He has a flip top and he's younger. Every morning he says to me, 'Baby, you're my little princess.'"

"He has no idea how old you are, does he?"

"Stop jiving, Jane."

"Sorry."

"Jane, listen, be careful with the money your father left us. Don't do anything stupid with it. You know he wouldn't have wanted you to waste it."

"Father is dead. He doesn't have an opinion on the money he left us."

"Don't flip your lid, Jane. I don't want us to go hungry, is all."

"We're not at war, Mother, we won't go hungry."

"Oh, I know that, Jane, but I don't know what I'd do without your help."

"You know full well that I invest the money in lucrative ventures. Your trip to Hawaii is proof of that, Mother— Sharon."

"Let's not talk about money, Jane, you know how I dislike it. I think it's in bad taste."

"What do you want to talk about?"

"Why don't you come to Hawaii and enjoy a drink on the beach? The men here are tanned and handsome."

"I dislike tanned people. They walk around with dead skin on their bodies."

"Gosh, Jane! You're always saying such strange and unfavorable things. Are you seeing anyone?"

"No."

"I figured. You've got that voice."

"What voice, Mother?"

"Sharon."

"What voice, Sharon?"

"The voice that single women have, Jane. You know very well what I'm talking about."

"No, I don't. I have to go. Enjoy your new acquisition."

"What do you mean? I haven't bought anything."

"You know very well what I mean, Mother."

Jane hung up.

She tied her bathrobe and lay down on the couch. She wanted a cigarette but she'd left them in her room. Staring up at the ceiling, she thought of the men she'd dated, and their derrières, none of which she could remember. She couldn't even remember the derrière of the only boyfriend she'd ever had. She remembered John, whose job was to take photographs for identity cards. He had small hands, toy hands. And he smelled like cabbage. He'd tried to kiss her on their second date, after calling her Stella, and this after Jane had told him several times that her name was not Stella. She remembered Bob's high-pitched voice, which was like the voice of a woman losing hers. He'd taken her to an Italian restaurant and ordered chicken and a salad to share. He worked at a candy factory, and during the date the only thing he talked about was the different ways of making all the candy that existed on the market, and how to produce all the candy that didn't yet exist but that would exist in the near future because he would take charge of bringing it into existence. When Jane asked him why he loved his work so much (as well as the word *existence* and variations thereof), he answered that he didn't love it but that he couldn't talk about anything else. And she remembered Mike, her only boyfriend. He'd left her for an exotic dancer who spoke French and worked as a librarian. She used cheap perfume and wore a pendant with a gold cross. Jane had always thought of her as the principal representative of an association that could be called Cruelty Devotees. Mike abhorred crosses because they were instruments of torture, though apparently he didn't abhor them enough. She remembered the most ridiculous things, but not the derrières.

The doorbell rang. Jane knew it was Carrie. She'd locked the door because Carrie would be stopping by at some point, with her refreshments and air kisses. She didn't get up. She didn't have the energy for Carrie and let the doorbell ring. Like all machines, Carrie was programmed—to go on visits. If she didn't, her internal cog would begin to rust. That's why she rang the doorbell for five minutes, believing that in this way, someone would replace absent Jane and there would be no conflict with her internal programming. Jane enjoyed the moment, she enjoyed the only revenge she occasionally allowed herself. Carrie wouldn't know what to do with her free time, with time that couldn't be used for a visit, and Jane gloated with pleasure. She imagined Carrie's head short-circuiting, and colored smoke spouting from her ears, and her bulging eyes spinning endlessly.

When Carrie left, Jane went back to her room.

She looked at herself in the mirror. Why didn't she act like a person with money? She didn't know. Nor did she know why she was incapable of taking the bills she made to the shopping mall and acquiring ten fish tanks with tropical fish, or the complete collection of Shirley Temple dolls, or glasses to make martinis next to the pool she didn't have, but should purchase. Along with a useless pet. A Chihuahua. That she'd call Ralph. She and Ralph would dress in sailor suits and matching hats. These were the things that people with money did. These were the things that her mother, Sharon, did. Jane thought she should go to Honolulu and collect hats in the colors of the drinks she would sip by the pool while her mother, Sharon, auctioned off the man with the best tan, whom she would deliver dressed as a sailor, just like Ralph. But Jane didn't have the energy for this, she just didn't. And she knew why she didn't have the energy for a canine freak dressed like Shirley Temple or for men with collectible derrières. She abhorred people with money. But she went on making it because it was the only way for her to stop thinking about the shadows of things and about her head filling with gray smoke and freezing in space.

She decided to go with the black outfit. It was too formal for a doctor's appointment, but it gave her the air of a businesswoman, of someone who uses her time to produce statistics and complex numbers that no one understands but that everyone admires. She tied her hair back with a green elastic and chose gold earrings that matched her glasses. She looked normal, she looked like someone who didn't feel that Manhattan's light had perforated her brain.

III

The secretary gave Jane a sidelong glance. She had taken a seat at the far end of the waiting room and opened a book that she wasn't reading. She was too nervous to think clearly. After lighting a cigarette, she looked around for an ashtray. There was one on the opposite end of a table. It was white, oval, alive. She paused. There was a plant close to her and she preferred to use it so she wouldn't have to get close to the ashtray. Why had she made the appointment? The secretary was savoring a piece of chewing gum, chomping on it with the rhythm of a cow chewing cud, but she was young, beautiful, made up. The rhythm, in this woman, was sensual. Jane would have liked to be a businesswoman with money who could laugh at women like this. But I am a businesswoman with money, Jane thought. I'm simply incapable of being a sensual deer. This was the image Jane had formed over the years—the prototype of what men looked for in women. An orphaned deer at the mercy of evil hunters who, on being rescued by a brave young man in a blue cape, would turn into Betty Boop and sing "Boop-Oop-a-Doop." Jane always arrived at the same dilemma: sensual deer need to be maintained and protected, but she had enough money and was insured against everything. She lived in an apartment with exposed bricks in Manhattan and had insurance against termites. What's more, she thought Betty Boop was deformed. She had macrocephaly. Jane had looked the word up in the dictionary. Betty Boop's head was disproportionately big and her mouth too small. In any case, what did *Boop-Oop-a-Doop* even mean?

The sensual cow answered the phone. Without getting up, she said, "Dr. Wesselmann is waiting for you. Would you please go in, ma'am?"

Jane didn't answer. Would she please? She felt the secretary's tone was rude. She put away her book, then thought
twice and took it out of her bag. With the book in her hand,
she felt less nervous.

Dr. Wesselmann greeted her with a smile.

"Miss Rosenquist? Pleased to meet you."

"Likewise."

"You're reading Faulkner? An exceptional book, isn't it?
One of my favorites."

Jane was unable to respond. She sat down silently, clutching the book to her chest. Her dress would be white, with
small lilac flowers on it. He'd choose the church, because he
was a widower. They'd have two children, Benjy and Quentin.
Then a girl, Caddy. They would explain that their children's
names had been chosen in honor of the book that had led to
their falling in love. People would look at them with admiration. They'd live in the New York suburbs in a home with a big
backyard and a swimming pool where Benjy would have a little
tree house, Quentin would dress up as a cowboy, and Caddy
would trot around on a pony with black spots. He'd teach her
to play golf, and she'd make strawberry pie and lemonade
on warm afternoons. They'd have long arguments about the
unfortunate behavior of her mother, Sharon, and with a kiss,
he'd say, "That's just the way she is, my love, you know that,"
and they'd laugh together.

"Are you feeling well, Miss Rosenquist?"

"Yes, of course, pardon me."

She would have liked to show him everything she'd jotted down in the book's margins, to talk to him about all the nights she'd wanted to read entire paragraphs to someone, to him, but she remained silent. She felt her face burning and was pleased to remember that the layer of makeup would cover her shame.

"What brings you here?"

Benjy, Quentin, and Caddy would wake them up on Sunday mornings with hot chocolate and cookies they'd baked the day before. Caddy would show them her drawings, Benjy would tell them about the new insects he'd found in the backyard, and Quentin, his hair tousled, would listen keenly, smiling.

"I have problems, with my vision, I think."

"What do you mean exactly? Are you losing your vision?"

He would be her confidant, and when his workday was over, she'd be waiting for him on the porch with a glass of cold beer and he'd ask, "How was your day, my little princess?" She'd tell him about the children's adventures, and about how the gray smoke was gone for good. He'd hug her and say, "I'm so happy to hear that, baby girl. You're my baby girl, do you know that?"

"No, that's not exactly it. Something that might be strange happens to me. That's how I can explain it, as something strange. I feel like Manhattan has perforated my brain and that things are alive."

"I don't follow you."

"How can we be sure this ashtray isn't really alive? I'm afraid of the shadows that things project. The shadows of things impact my face and leave small bruises."

"Uh-huh."

He would never have said "uh-huh," not if they'd had three kids and a porch.

"This is what happens to me. When I light a cigarette, my brain fills with gray smoke. I imagine the smoke escaping through holes in my brain, transforming into opaque crystals that fly through the air and accumulate, eventually choking me. There's that and the shadows of objects. And the sense that they're alive. I feel . . . damaged. And it's not something that can be fixed with a vacation to Hawaii."

"I understand."

But he didn't. Jane pressed her fingers into the book.

"Have you tried sedatives? There's a very effective drug called Valium."

"I don't need drugs."

"Of course not, it's just a suggestion."

"Did you know that Faulkner wrote in boiler rooms because one of his jobs was taking care of boilers, and that he was a pilot in the British Royal Air force, and that he worked as a painter of roofs and doors, and that he was the postman at a university, and that . . . ?"

"Sure, of course. Here's the Valium prescription. If you have any problems give my secretary a call and have her schedule another appointment. It was a pleasure to meet you."

But his pleasure was not strong enough for Benjy to go to university, for Quentin to travel the world, and for Caddy to become a deer hunter.

Jane got to her feet slowly. She took the prescription and let it hang from her hand. She didn't know what to do with it. He walked her to the door and sent her off with a little push.

The secretary gave Jane her invoice. Then she blew a bubble with her chewing gum and it burst in her face. She looked at Dr. Wesselmann and smiled. But he wasn't looking at her, so she placed her hand gently on his shoulder, batted her eyelashes, and said, "Sorry, Doctor." He patted her derrière and bit his lips. She laughed and winked. When he left, the secretary looked at Jane and muttered, "Is there anything else?" She said this ruminating, her chewing gum moving to the rhythm of "Boop-Oop-a-Doop."

Jane felt like a wounded doe, a doe agonizing in silence.

IV

She left the office, went straight to the shopping mall, and bought the biggest, most expensive, most useless dishwasher she could find.

V

". . . and everyone is saying that Mrs. Hamilton was seen with Mr. Odelmburg. The nerve of that woman! How dare she? She just got divorced. A woman always has to keep up appearances, especially if she's a divorcée. My husband told me she was a slut. An amoral woman."

"Hi, Carrie."

Carrie took out the refreshments and placed them on a shallow dish. "New dishwasher?"

"Yes. I bought it when I left the office."

"Which office?"

"Dr. Wesselmann's office."

Carrie choked on the refreshment and started to cough. She took a sip of lemonade and shouted, "Jeez, Jane! Why didn't you tell me you saw Dr. Wesselmann? He's so seductive, so handsome, isn't he?"

Carrie's eyes were going crazy. They opened and closed uncontrollably. She began to give Jane little pats. She thought that Carrie's pats were the vertical equivalent of her air kisses. She reckoned the machine was about to collapse and regretted that it didn't.

"When are you having dinner together?"

"Never."

"Oh, Jane! I'm so sorry. At least you have your dishwasher, right?"

"Uh-huh."

"Did he prescribe something for the problems with your vision?"

"Valium."

"Isn't that a drug for . . . ?"

"For?"

"Crazies."

"Yes, it is."

Carrie got up, looked for her things, and left. Jane never would have imagined that machines could panic. What a pity, she thought, no air kisses this time.

She went to the kitchen, folded the Valium prescription, and placed it in a glass. Then she turned on the dishwasher and put the glass with the prescription inside it.

She looked for her cigarettes and went about observing, in ecstasy, the infinite, many-colored crystals accumulating in the air.

# EARTH

The earth is burning me. It isn't dry. It's burning me because it's hot out. The sun is draining the water from the earth little by little. Papá is down below. My bare feet are on the earth and they hurt; my feet are on top of Papá. I took off my shoes, threw them away because I was hot, and now I can't find them. I want it to be night so everything cools down and I can lie close to Papá, though really I'll be far from him, because I'm higher up.

He always wanted me close. "Camila, where are you going? Come here, I'm calling you."

"I'm coming, Mamá wants me to help her with the dishes."

"I don't want you washing dishes, not a single dish, you're to have the hands of a little lady. Your mother can do them herself."

Mamá turned the tap all the way on. The water knocked over the pile of plates, but she didn't care if they broke.

She stopped looking at me. That was at first, when Papá just wanted me close. Later, after what happened, she stopped talking to me. She sat in her rocking chair and stared at a point on the wall.

"What are you looking at, Mamá?"

"Leave your mother in peace, Camila. Come here, Papá wants to show you something."

Mamá went still, her chair went still. She stared at the point on the wall and it was like she was going to disappear, she had gone so still, and so white.

Now I want to stare at a point on the wall and rock back and forth, but I can't because the sun is burning my head and my eyes hurt. I have to close them, like I did when Papá came into my room.

No one leaves flowers in this abandoned place. It's the cemetery with the black gate, the one really far from town. It's so far that Mamá spent all her savings on the wagon and two men she rented to bring him here. It took two days. Papá has no cross or flowers, but I made him a flower out of a piece of newspaper I found on the ground. Betty taught me how to make paper flowers. And birds. She came over to drink maté with Mamá. When I was little she brought me candies and markers that we always used to color with. But after that day, when I walked through the kitchen and Betty was there talking to Mamá, she went quiet, the two of them went quiet. One day I told Mamá that I was going to the convenience store, but I didn't leave. I hid under the kitchen table. Nobody could see me because I was covered by the tablecloth. Not long after, Betty came over.

"Is the brat here?"

"No, she went to the convenience store."

"What are you going to do, Norita?"

"I don't know."

"When did you see them?"

"A month ago."

"Did they see you?"

"No, I don't think so."

"It's just going to get worse."

"I know."

"Report him."

"He'll kill me."

There was a long silence, I thought I heard Mamá crying.

The black dress is bugging me. Mamá made me wear it the day Papá died. I didn't want to go with her. She set the black dress down on my bed and told me to put it on. But not with words. She stood in the door frame and looked at me until I did. The earth is drying out, but it's still soft. There are ants and beetles on it. It's fun to kill the ants. The beetles gross me out. I get tired of standing and sit down. I don't care if the dress gets dirty, because it doesn't matter. The ants form a trail that ends in a little hole in the ground. I put leaves, twigs, pebbles in front of them so they can't follow their trail, so they have to crawl over things. Some of them get lost, it's like they don't understand, but after a while they find the trail and disappear into the hole. Papá used to make me stand for a long time. I complained at first, told him it hurt, said I didn't like it, but he looked at me and smiled and covered my mouth and kept going. The red ants are biting me, so I kill them.

I'm hungry and thirsty. "Mamá, I'm thirsty." Mamá used to get the glass pitcher out of the fridge and slowly pour me some water. It made a noise that lasted the whole time the glass filled with water, and little drops splashed all over the table. I used to go up to her and stand next to the table so the drops would sprinkle onto my face. Mamá would look at me, smile, and kiss them away. This was when I was really little, when Papá traveled a lot, when he was almost never home. Then he was fired and he stopped traveling. A beetle wants to crawl over my foot and I let it. But then I flick it off. I wish I had the garden poison Mamá uses to kill all the insects. The sun hits the beetle's wings and it looks like it's many different colors. I want it to leave my foot in peace, but it keeps crawling onto me.

Mamá went off with the men. She left me here, in the cemetery with the black gate. They dug a hole in the earth, put Papá in it, and covered him up. Mamá told the men to wait in the wagon, to give us a bit of time alone. When they were far away, she looked at the dark earth and spat on it. Then she spat on me. I stood there, not understanding. After that, she left. I wanted to follow her, but when I ran up to her she took me by the hair, dragged me back to Papá's grave, and pushed me onto the damp earth. When I was able to stand, she was already in the wagon. I ran, but I couldn't reach her.

That was yesterday and I know she's not coming back. I know this because when Papá died, I hid under the kitchen table.

Mamá said to Betty, "I'm going to take him far away, to the cemetery with the black gate."

"Why so far?"

"Because I can't bear the thought of him being close."

"But it's going to cost you a lot, Norita. Renting a wagon and the men to help you for a two-day trip."

"I don't care."

"What are you going to do with the girl?"

There was a long silence. "I can't bear the thought of having her close either."

"But she's your daughter."

"Not anymore, not after what happened."

"It's not her fault."

"Yes, it is."

"I don't understand, Norita. She's a victim."

"No, she isn't. She's dangerous."

After I heard that I didn't understand anything, like right now, with the sun burning my body and making it hard to breathe. Two beetles start climbing up my leg and I shake them off. There are no trees nearby, just grass. I cover my feet with the earth, I stick them into it to feel the damp, so the sun stops burning them, so the beetles go away.

Everything was better when Papá wasn't around. When he came back, I just wanted him to leave me in peace, like with these bugs that won't stop bothering me. Mamá knows what I did, that's why she left me here. She thinks I could do the same thing to her, but I'd never do anything to her. I just wanted to be with her. I just wanted her to stop crying. But it doesn't matter now. I stick an arm under the earth and leave it there, feeling the damp, far from the sun's heat. One day, the day Papá died, he was in my room. He asked me for a glass of wine.

"Camila, go get me some more wine. Hurry up, the bottle's empty."

"I'll ask Mamá because the wine is on the top shelf in the cupboard and I can't reach."

"No, don't ask your mamá anything. Go get a bench and get the wine down right now."

I went to the kitchen, pulled the bench over to the cupboard, and got the wine. When I went to look for a glass, I saw that Mamá had forgotten the insect poison on the kitchen table. I put three spoonfuls in and stirred it, like with sugar. I gave him the glass and he finished it in one gulp. He looked at me strangely, as if he knew. He grabbed his throat, turned red, yelled a little, and fell to the floor. I stood there watching his face get redder and redder, swell bigger and bigger. He was trembling and it was like he wasn't going to stop. But then he went still.

Mamá came into the room without looking at me. "You killed him."

"Yes."

She didn't say anything, just looked at Papá, and it was like she wanted to speak, but no words came out.

"I didn't want to, Mamá, but he hurt me. He made you cry."

"Shut up. Help me get him into bed."

I helped her carry him to the bed and, when he was in it, I started to cry.

"Shut up, you little shit. This is your fault. You killed my husband."

I couldn't stop crying, I couldn't say anything to her.

"Today it's my husband, tomorrow it could be someone else."

I didn't understand her, I just wanted her to look at me again, to kiss away my tears. Mamá didn't talk to me after that. She convinced the town that her husband had died from a heart attack. Everyone believed her, no one asked any questions, no one suspected anything. I don't know what she said about me. Maybe people think I escaped.

My legs are under the earth, I don't feel them anymore. Both of my arms and the rest of my body are sinking into it. Red ants are crawling over my face. I don't want to kill them, I can't. The sun doesn't bother me anymore because it's almost night. A beetle is climbing up my neck. The ants are crawling over my eyes, following a trail that feels like it's never going to end. They don't stop. The earth is still damp.

I'm getting closer and closer to Papá.

# PERFECT SYMMETRY

*— For Gonzalo Bazterrica —*

He moved the sieve. Flour fell onto the yolks, dotting the yellow liquid with white. He didn't let his mind make the obvious analogies about snow and cold and freedom, and he focused on the circular motion of the sieve. The spots covered the yellow surface with a precise rhythm. He smiled. Then he picked up a glass pitcher and poured out a bit of cold milk. As he whisked the liquid, the yellow disappeared into the white flour and milk. Its thickness gave way, forming a light batter. The milk smells fragile, he thought, and the word surprised him. He picked up the pitcher and brought it to his nose. For a few seconds, he inhaled the smell, but he couldn't retain it or determine whether it was sweet or bitter or a mix of the two. It's because it's cold, he thought, the cold diffuses smells, encapsulates them.

He went over to the fridge and struggled with the door, the sudden movement causing some of the milk to spill from the pitcher. He looked at the white drops on the black floor and thought he could make out a design, a Chinese design, a dragon. It wasn't perfect, but there it was, with wings and white fire coming out of its open mouth. He left the pitcher in the fridge. That night, they killed him.

He took three eggs out of the fridge and pushed the door shut with his elbow. Only he didn't push hard enough and it swung back open. He walked over to the counter and placed the eggs in a shallow dish, then went back for the butter. He thought he'd put it away, but saw it on the wooden countertop. His fingers had left an imprint in the packaging. It was hot outside, and the fridge's cool air hadn't hardened it enough. Soft butter seemed unnatural to him. He knew this was illogical because, if anything, butter was naturally soft, but its greasy consistency, which made it hard to handle, bothered him. He needed the small rectangles, the vertical, calculated cut, that cold butter offered. He went back to the fridge and shoved the door shut. He looked for the dragon on the floor. For a second, he thought he saw a claw sliding along the drain, but the dragon wasn't there, it had become dirty water. He walked over to the counter, picked up the eggs, and, one by one, placed them in a pot of boiling water.

Twenty-seven had him marked. He never learned when or how, but he knew the man had ordered him killed. He knew there was a problem the night nobody let him sit at their table. It all became clear when they stopped talking to him. When the guards stopped cursing him, he knew he was a lost cause.

He added some butter to a hot pan—with a spoon. A knife seemed inappropriate, given the butter's lack of consistency. He moved the pan in circles until the butter covered the surface. With another spoon, a bigger one, he added the semiliquid mixture consisting of egg yolks, milk, and flour. He covered the pan with this batter so that it formed a perfect white circle. Then he waited, and when the top had darkened, forming a crepe, he moved the pan in such a way that it became unstuck, flipped in the air, and landed back in the same spot. When it was ready, he slid it onto a plate. He picked up the spoon and repeated the procedure with another portion of batter. When the crepe landed in the pan, after its flawless flight, he smiled.

Twenty-seven was ruthless. From the day he'd been marked by the man, he was treated like a stranger, like something without value. He didn't mind being ignored; he preferred the silence. What he couldn't accept was the restriction Twenty-seven had ordered on the only space where he experienced well-being and pleasure. Forbidding him from entering the kitchen had been an open and brutal declaration of war. It was for this reason that he wasn't surprised by how easy it had been to obtain a transfer to the ward where the infected were kept. The guards always gave those who'd been marked by Twenty-seven a final wish. It was a tacit rule, one everyone knew about and respected. He hadn't requested the transfer to escape, as he knew Twenty-seven was not subject to restrictions.

He sliced the ham into triangles, rounding one side so it would align with the crepe's circular edge. The knife was sharp, it made the job easier. He should have been using a plastic knife, but the guard understood it didn't matter. If anything, many of them would celebrate his killing Twenty-seven, if he managed it, so the guard hid a sharp knife for him. He placed the triangles of ham on the crepe, then removed the eggs from the boiling water and peeled them.

He'd spent everything on this night. The day before, he'd given the guard three books to sell, some money, and his last cigarettes to buy the ingredients he needed to cook. He would have liked to make another dish, something more elaborate, but he knew he'd been lucky. The guard had taken pity on him and had obtained a few things, the basics. They were sufficient to prepare a decent dish. With this money, I could get you a cheap girl, something better than the shit you're asking for. That's what the guard had told him after seeing the list of ingredients. He hadn't responded. He knew that no woman was cheap and that every dish was delicious. The secret was in the particulars that made them unique. The guard gave him a look of bewildered disgust, but brought him the things on the list.

He thought he saw a shadow. He waited, alert, for a few seconds. Nothing, it was nothing.

He'd requested the transfer to the ward for the infected so he could cook. He needed to do this at night, while everyone was asleep. He needed to do it with precision. He'd wanted access to a space where he could be alone, to the freedom granted by silence. They let him do what he wished, without restrictions. What they needed was a result: dead or triumphant. Both options were valid.

The stuffed triangles were ready. He placed them in the pan with hot oil. The oil's transparency surprised him, as did being able to observe the cooking process closely as a result. He always felt he was in the presence of a living entity when he heard the sound of hot oil. Far from startling him, it fascinated him. He thought that oil, over fire, transformed into a being, into something that would likely never die, that simply learned to remain hidden, in wait. He went to get the basil leaves to wash them. First he smelled them, and the scent pleased him. The feeling was simple and fleeting. He remembered that the scent of cinnamon had a similar effect on him. He was indifferent to its taste, but its scent, its scent could turn his morning around, his mood. He turned on the tap and placed the leaves one by one under the stream of cold water. As he washed each leaf with care, he looked closely at its structure. The pure, compact color of the upper part contrasted with the fragility of the grayish green underside. He wondered if there was any life left in them, if they could feel his fingers cleaning them, slowly, carefully. Under the water, the green intensified, and he played with the thought that this could be true, that the leaves could feel.

Death was a pastime for Twenty-seven. He enjoyed killing. He boasted of being silent and of attacking when it was least expected. Just like real death, he said. The terror his victims felt clouded the comprehension and lucidity needed to realize that Twenty-seven's tactics were basic, primitive. And it was this terror, which Twenty-seven cultivated and amplified, that made him effective. There was pleasure, an infinite pleasure, in knowing that others feared him, that they would try to escape, that they would give anything to be absolved. He knew that Twenty-seven hadn't been able to handle his lack of reaction, the fact that he hadn't pleaded. And he knew that for this reason the attack would be planned, hermetic, and savage.

He would have liked to open a bottle of wine at that moment. He missed good wine. A Malbec to sip on while he cooked, a Merlot with his meal. He liked to raise a glass of wine by its long stem, to get a sense of the crystal's apparent lightness. And to observe the red color offering a new view of things, its aroma transforming the core of beings. When he moved the glass slowly, the wine's elongated shapes grew. These were what the experts called legs, a term he refused to use. He felt it was limited, given the number of universes he'd discovered in a glass of wine. He missed the dimensions of wine, the worlds.

There would be no Malbec tonight, but he remembered a harvest from '95. He'd sampled it before losing his freedom. He remembered the well-rounded flavor in his mouth, time stopping in the soft wood, the water motionless in the grapes, the dry and complex wind that defined the wine's body. He smiled.

The golden-brown triangles were ready. He set them on a clean white plate, one next to the other, leaving a spotless half centimeter between them. He placed the basil leaves to the left of the triangles, forming a solid green circle. Then he scattered ground black pepper along the upper edge of the plate.

He heard a noise and instinctively grabbed the knife. He walked around the kitchen. Nothing. No one. He returned to the counter and focused on the plate. Something was missing, more color. Definition. He thought of the ingredients he had left, yellow was the only color he could use. He looked for the knife to slice an egg and remove the yolk. He couldn't find it.

He was still. He didn't care if he died. With his eyes closed, he thought of the cool, smooth basil leaves in his fingers, imagined the crispy sound of the crepe being sliced, the taste of the ingredients fusing to expand in his mouth, their smell caressing him, their colors captivating him.

Then he was grabbed from behind. He didn't move, and in swift silence, they cut his throat. He opened his eyes and saw three drops of blood, his blood, fall symmetrically onto the lower edge of the plate, balancing the dish's composition, making his work unique, perfect.

He fell with his eyes open, and a look that resembled a smile.

# THE WOLF'S BREATH

The wolf is restless behind the glass that surrounds it. The wolf bites. A dense spiderweb of tiny particles forms in the air that encloses it: the light water borne of its breath. Because the wolf is restless. Behind the glass. And it bites.

The wolf looks like a man dressed in black on a street corner. But facing you is a wolf who wants to devour you. A dark claw will swipe through moist air, glass will be licked until it shatters. The wolf will kill you.

It will devour you with its thoughts, find the sweet spot to savor you. It will measure your breath, calculate the exact moment to brush your veins with its fangs, to embrace you gently with its mouth.

You want to slip away from the dream, from the glass that obscures your vision, from this transparent and human animal. You don't want to bear witness to the fragility of a moment, the tepidness of life, the lightness of a body. You don't want to be part of a savage banquet. But you intuit that each of us is a wolf devouring the other in exquisite eternity. A wolf that does so with the subtle delicacy of bites that flow like caresses over skin being maimed. That slip like lights inside drops, like drops inside glass, like glass containing a wolf, a wolf that looks like a man on a corner.

Who's going to kill you.

# TEICHER VS. NIETZSCHE

*— For Mariano Borobio —*

Teicher woke, resolved to kick Nietzsche that morning. He was frenetic. Boca was playing River in the Apertura Tournament's deciding match. This fact deserved to be celebrated with a bloody kick. Teicher walked to the kitchen, found Nietzsche seated there, and calculated the distance from foot to head. Teicher would have to strike Nietzsche between the eyes, thereby stunning him for several hours so he wouldn't disrupt the match. Teicher focused by summoning Seppaquercia's midfield goal from back in '79, which had been scored five seconds after the start of the match against Huracán. He yelled, "Gooooaaaal, carajo!" Nietzsche gave him a sidelong glance and, in a masterful move, evaded the crazed foot with a single bound, landing next to his food dish. He commenced eating. In the process of kicking Nietzsche, which had been drawn out unnecessarily due to his prior preparations, Teicher, shocked by their subsequent failure, lost his balance and fell abruptly to the floor. He hit it with such force that it took him a while to react. When he did, he realized he couldn't move. He felt a sharp pain along the length of his spine. Nietzsche continued to eat, impassively, without looking at him.

Nietzsche had received a formidable number of nicknames over the course of his life. Friedrich Wilhelm Nietzsche for formal introductions: "Allow me to introduce Friedrich Wilhelm Nietzsche, we're proud of him"; Friedrich for neutral moments: "Not now, Friedrich, come back later"; Nichi for affectionate moments: "Sweet Nichi, what beautiful whiskers you have, Nichi"; Bad Nichito when he was being scolded: "Bad Nichito, don't eat the plants"; Nichi Nuchito for moments of crazed love: "Nichi Nuchito, I love you, I love you, I love you, I love you." His ex-wife had repeated this series of nicknames, proud of her mediocre inventiveness. Teicher didn't call Nietzsche by any name. Theirs was a relationship based on convenience; they ignored each other. This tacit agreement worked until the day his ex-wife left him. After that it was inevitable. Nietzsche for formal introductions: "This is Nietzsche. Do you like him? Please take him with you"; Demented-Schizophrenic-Lunatic when Teicher was angry: "Demented-Schizophrenic-Lunatic, don't destroy the books!"; Stupid Ball for neutral moments: "Stupid Ball, your existence is useless"; Worthless Object for rainy days: "Worthless Object, why aren't you an umbrella?"; Syphilitic Filth for philosophical moments: "Syphilitic Filth, the eternal return was created so I'll always be able to kick you."

There were two things Teicher had never understood. The first and most important was why his ex-wife had abandoned him. Not *him*, he didn't care about that, but that animate thing with hair. The second was why she had chosen the name Nietzsche, and not one worthy of the creature's volatile mind, such as Fluffy or Pussycat. It wasn't possible that she fully comprehended Nietzsche's philosophy, so the name couldn't have been an homage. Though he suspected that his ex-wife possessed a concentrated sordidness that coexisted happily with her monumental simplicity and uselessness. Her name was Elisabeth, just like the philosopher's sister. Of the immense richness that emanated from a figure such as Nietzsche, she had chosen this aspect, his unhealthy relationship with his sister, Elisabeth, and not something more lighthearted, such as the creature's resemblance to him, because of their whiskers, and this produced so great an aversion in Teicher that he considered killing Nietzsche, embalming him, and after this pleasurable process, mailing him to his ex-wife so that she could finally carry out zoophilic and necrophiliac incest.

Teicher was still lying on the repugnant kitchen floor, helpless. His head hurt. It had struck the edge of the table when he'd fallen. He tried to move but couldn't manage it. He couldn't feel his legs and wanted to shout, and also cry, though he wouldn't allow himself. Instead, he made a series of mental notes: "Hire someone to clean the floor, urgent," "Kill Nietzsche," "Lift the furniture, recover all the supposedly lost objects," "Kill Nietzsche," "Go back to the gym, get in shape, and successfully kick this nauseating creature once and for all." He saw a cockroach crawl out from under the fridge; he saw it stop in the middle of the kitchen, move its antennae, climb onto the table, and walk around the cold beer, sandwich, and fries, before getting lost in a chunk of Roquefort. The cockroach had some nerve, and Teicher felt this to be an insult to his condition as a predatory football-playing mammal.

The match would be on in ten minutes, and before the apocalyptic flying kick, Teicher had carried out a ritual. He'd gotten out of bed with his right foot; he'd walked to the bathroom reciting the lineup; he'd showered using only his right hand; he'd sung crowd favorites like "Boca is my life and joy, Boca, you're the tops in Argentina, you chase Racing and Las Gallinas, you chase El Cuervo and the police, let's go, Bo, let's go, Bo"; on the fogged-up window, he'd written "Come on, Xeneizes, let's do this!"; he'd put on the regulation jersey he'd bought when Boca had won the Supercopa in '89, and the briefs and socks full of holes he wore for all their matches; he'd prepared his food systematically, the food he always ate, in the same order, and the same proportions; he'd isolated the house from external sounds, closing blinds and windows, because absolute concentration was required; he'd turned the television on and clicked to the appropriate channel. Boca could not, under any circumstances, in any situation, lose this match. He was certain that if the team failed to win, it would disrupt the energetic harmony of the superstitious rituals that football fans had refined over centuries. He tried to drag himself along the floor, but any movement made him shout in pain. His desired destinations—the phone and the couch—were at an abysmal distance. He lay there on his back, looking at the ceiling.

To calm himself down, he began to recite Boca's international titles: "the 1977 Copa Libertadores, the 1978 Copa Libertadores, the 1978 Copa Intercontinental, the 1989 Supercopa de América, the 1990 Recopa Sudamericana . . ." Nietzsche, who was strolling around the house, decided to walk over Teicher's chest, evidence that he didn't consider this human's body to be an obstacle, or recognize its presence. Teicher yelled, "Parasitic assassin of God . . . ," and choked. At that moment, he knew that God was indeed dead, because no god, or group of gods, or even a simple demiurge could approve of a punishment like this. The evidence of this affirmation terrified him. Such was the brutality of what was happening to him that the only fathomable possibility was a lethal virus, one capable of liquidating all the celestial hordes, including the sweet and sticky winged cherubim. God was dead, and he knew that if Boca didn't win, there wouldn't be many opportunities for God, or Jesus, or the Holy Trinity to be resurrected because he would take responsibility for assassinating them as many times as was necessary. Nietzsche ran his tail over Teicher's face and Teicher automatically did nothing; he decided to ignore this act that, though disrespectful, hadn't—and this was thanks to his infinite compassion—led to an attempt at exterminating Nietzsche, at least not yet.

In the middle of these thoughts, Teicher lost consciousness. When he came to, he didn't know where he was. He was so dazed after his fall that he couldn't think clearly—until he saw Nietzsche, dangerously close, staring at him, wearing a grin of sorts, as though he were secretly pleased to see him in this degrading situation. Teicher looked at the clock in the kitchen and let out a yelp. The match would be over in five minutes. The pain could not be an impediment. He had to reach the living room. He hadn't missed a single match in his entire life.

He thought of colossal players like Silvio Marzolini, Rojitas, Antonio Roma, El Leoncito Pescia, El Loco Gatti, Roberto Mouzo, and in honor of these luminaries, he made a superhuman effort to drag himself across the floor. The pain took his breath away. To concentrate, he repeated in his head, "I love you, Boca, I'd rather die than be a Gallina." When he reached the door to the living room and stretched his neck into it, he heard Borobio commenting on the end of the match: "Here we are at the mythic Bombonera Stadium in the neighborhood of La Boca, at none other than the classic of classics, Boca-River, and we're reaching the end of the match. A match that's had it all, two goals a team, headers, penalties, goals from outside the box, players sent off, and an incredible atmosphere. This match, at this stadium, should be at the top of the list of sporting events to see before you die. But let's get back to the action. It's two goals apiece and Diablo Monserrat has the ball, River attacks, River wants to take this under the wire, Monserrat goes down the right wing, dodges Pineda, passes to center, header from Salas, and El Mono Navarro Montoya blocks the shot! This match is gonna give us all a heart attack. El Mono is quick with a long ball to midfield, the Uruguayan Cedrés brings the ball down, Ayala marks him and fouls him. Yellow card for Ayala and a free kick for Boca. This could be the last ball of the night. We're at full time. Bilardo, Boca's manager, sends everyone into the box. It's there that El Tweety Carrario, Cedrés, and Guerra wait. The center backs also move forward, La Tota Fabbri and El Negro Cáceres will try for the winning header. Now Boca wants to give this a final go and take all the glory, the team's putting all the meat on the barbecue. The referee gives the order, Mauricio Pineda kicks the ball into the box, the Uruguayan Hugo Romeo Guerra jumps for it between River's defenders, he heads the ball from behind, beating his markers, and . . ."

And Nietzsche, who was lying on the couch, leaped onto the remote control and turned off the television.

For a second, Teicher didn't understand what was happening. Then, stunned, he felt a sudden, sharp pain in his left arm that moved into his chest. He knew these were the symptoms of a heart attack. He understood he was going to die of rage, of helplessness, of pain, and that he was never going to learn the result of the match. Nietzsche ran his tail over Teicher's face and sauntered philosophically toward the kitchen.

Before he died, Teicher was certain of two things. First, he was finally able to comprehend why his ethereal and sordid ex-wife had chosen a name that held so much weight for an insignificant cat. Second, and more important, he understood why she had abandoned Nietzsche. The eternal return would ensure that Nietzsche's simple and effective act of turning off the television, and consequently bringing about Teicher's death (the perfect homicide premeditated by his ex-wife), would be repeated time and time again.

# THE DEAD

*—  For Pilar Bazterrica  —*

All dead people go to the moon. When a body stiffens and gets cold it's because it knows that it's slowly going to turn into steam, like when water is really hot and lots of white steam rises to the ceiling. First it's the dead person's finger, then another finger, then their arm, and their head, until their whole body is trapped in some pit on the moon.

Mamá never explained about the dust in the drawer. But I know what it is. Once I went to Uncle Alberto's house and I ate Aunt Camelia's dust. Uncle Alberto kept it in a box that my papá said is called an urn. It tasted bad and left a stain. Uncle Alberto told me not to touch the urn, but I didn't care and I ate the dust in secret. Father Benito told me, and I believe him because he's a priest and priests are good and don't lie, that we're condemned to dust for our sins. He told me that being condemned is like going straight to hell. I think dust is the soul's filth, that's why coffins go under the earth, so the sins don't hurt anybody.

Mamá is on the moon and I miss her. She calls me and says, I want you to come here because the dead scare me. She tells me that they're all looking at something. Some of them look around, but it's like they don't see anything, like their eyes are full of nothing, but others look angry, so angry that Mamá cries and calls me. I miss her. I want to turn into steam, but I'm not dead. Mamá's voice is so pretty. Sometimes she sings to me.

Yesterday I decided I was going to go to the moon. I'd cut off one of my fingers and bury it in the garden. Then I'd cut off another one, and then my hand, my arm, my head, until my whole body was trapped in a pit on the moon and I could be with Mamá.

Papá hit me. He was looking for the knife to cut the meat and he found it in my room. What's this doing here? he said. I told him Mamá was yelling and that I had to go to the moon to be with her, but he hit me on my mouth. Shut up, you brat, what are you saying? He left and locked me in my room. Papá is bad. He hit me.

Now he's watching TV. He turned it on loud, so loud that the words get into my body. They want to cut my veins. They're bad like Papá. He's like a big black word that watches you. He's bad and he scares me. He for sure ate Aunt Camelia's dust and that's why he hit me. He for sure had some in secret and that's why he's so bad now.

It's strange that I haven't cut my body up. I haven't even cut my head off. It's because Uncle Alberto and Papá have been home. That's why I haven't been able to do it. I think Papá also misses Mamá. He cries sometimes, and drinks a lot, and then he has a lot of water in his body and cries more. When Papá has that much water in his body, he isn't a scary bad word. He's like a puppet in the park, the ones that look like they're always falling even though they never fall because they're held up by strings you can barely see. But Papá doesn't have any strings inside him and he really does fall. Though sometimes I think that he used to have strings, and that when Mamá died they were all cut.

The other day Papá wasn't that sad and he didn't cry that much. He came home without Uncle Alberto and with a lady. The lady had on a skirt like Mamá's, one with flowers in different colors, and Papá ran his hand through her hair, but not like he does with me, he touched her differently, more slowly. After that he came up to my room. I had gone up first and lain down in my clothes but I was still awake. Papá thought I was sleeping.

I got out of bed without making any noise and walked to the living room like I was floating. The lady was lying on the couch and her blond hair was on a cushion. Papá kissed her and this made me furious. I knew I had to go to sleep because it was late, but it's not my fault if I misbehave. Everything is Uncle Alberto's fault. He put Aunt Camelia's dust in that box and I had some. Now I have the filth of Aunt Camelia's soul stuck to my body, only on the inside. I want it to go away but I don't know how to clean inside me. One day I asked Papá what would happen if I drank holy water because Father Benito told me it cleans the soul's impurities. I didn't really understand the part about impurities, but I pictured holy water being like bleach and cleaning things you can't see. How could you even think of drinking that? Papá said. Don't talk nonsense. The TV was on. Loud. There were no words, but there were two policemen running, and they were shooting and yelling. The living room was dark, but with the light from the TV I could see the lady's blond hair, and sometimes it looked like it was black, because the light went away, but afterward, when it came back, it was long and blond again. I didn't like that hair, it moved strangely on the cushion, it wasn't like my hair or like Papá's hair, which is short and doesn't move. There were more shots and the lady took off her skirt that had all the flowers in different colors on it. She threw the skirt that was just like Mamá's on the floor. Papá didn't tell her to pick it up like when I throw my clothes on the floor. That made me furious. Then Papá tried to take her shirt off, but she said no. Papá and the lady looked like they were wet, like when you take a bath, but they weren't naked. The lady's shirt was on and Papá had his trousers on. It smelled like Aunt Camelia's dust. It looked like the lady's legs wanted to hurt Papá's head, but he didn't scream. Her legs were very long and white and they moved like her hair. I didn't like them, they looked like the legs of a giant insect, like the ones I see on TV. A white spider's legs. The lady was saying something to Papá in a quiet voice. Her voice wasn't like Mamá's at all. Mamá's voice is prettier. Papá kissed her some more times and grabbed her arms. Then he began to move forcefully and it was like the police on TV were shooting at him. One, two, three, and more bullets into Papá's body, and it didn't stop moving. Four, five, six, and more bullets into his back, his legs, his head. The spider started to cry. I thought it was because the police were shooting at Papá. But no, spiders aren't good, and they don't cry. Papá was still for a while and then he started to say things to her. She kept pretending to cry, but I knew she was faking it. After that, she screamed a little and I thought Papá had hurt her and I was glad. But then I got a little scared because I thought he'd turned into a black word that was really making her cry. I wasn't scared for her, for the spider, I was scared because I knew the black word could stick to me. Then they started to laugh and hug each other. The blanket fell to the floor. I didn't want to be good and cover them. The spider grossed me out.

Mamá doesn't sing to me anymore. She cries and yells. She says, I'm alone and I want Papá to hug me like when we were together. I don't remember what her hair was like anymore, it wasn't brown or blond, but kind of a mix of both colors. I can't remember because I think hair is like the soul's filth and that's why Mamá's hair is dust now. But her voice and the skin on her face and her eyes can't be dust. With all that, she for sure evaporated, but not her hair, which must be like the earth now, but a prettier color.

I told Papá that Mamá misses him. He ran his hand through my hair and told me that she was in heaven with the little angels, and very happy. I didn't like it when he did that because he wasn't looking and he messed up my hair. So then I said, and I was mad, No, Mamá yells and cries because she's alone on the moon, and she's cold, and she wants you to go there. Papá got a strange look on his face. He sat down on the couch and started to drink. It was like he wanted to cry but he couldn't because he hadn't had enough to drink yet. He looked at a photo of Mamá on the table and that was when I realized he was afraid of going to the moon. That's why I went to go look for the knife to cut the meat.

# ELENA-MARIE SANDOZ

. . . a single black spot made up of poverty
and consequently hunger, crime, and dirt.

—Thomas Bernhard

Elena-Marie Sandoz was buried in the Cemetery of the Silver Crosses. She'd been dumped in a derelict grave with no name, destined for outcasts. No one wanted to go near the Cemetery of the Silver Crosses at night because the graves were in *very bad shape*. The reason the graves were in *very bad shape* was unexpected, since there was a municipal commission responsible for their maintenance, which charged a monthly fee that everyone paid. However, in my opinion there was a subconscious reason no one *in effect* took responsibility for maintaining the graves. That reason, which lurked silently and covertly in everyone's minds, was the fear people have of graves that are in poor shape. Many people pay regular visits to the Cemetery of the Silver Crosses to add a bit of fear, as it were, to the monotony of their lives. People are capable of anything to dissipate the monotony of their lives.

They're capable of going to the Cemetery of the Silver Crosses and spending hours in front of graves in bad shape to try to see if something is growing or *moving* inside them. But when night approaches, these people flee to hide in the monotonous reality of their lives. When Elena-Marie Sandoz was buried in the Cemetery of the Silver Crosses, I didn't visit her grave because I was afraid that her image, that is, the *singular* image I had in my mind of Elena-Marie Sandoz, would come undone and mix with the fear people deposit in the Cemetery of the Silver Crosses when they flee to take refuge in the monotony of reality. Elena-Marie Sandoz wasn't my wife, my lover, my girlfriend, my sister, my mother, or my teacher. She wasn't *anyone* to me for a long time. Not until the day I saw her in the movie *Eyes of Pain*, a movie that was screened twice at the municipal community theater. *Eyes of Pain* was screened only twice because no one was *really* interested in a badly acted B movie, a deplorable production with a weak, poorly constructed plot. The municipal community theater was ready to stop showing *Eyes of Pain* after the first screening because the audience had left silently until it was practically empty. At no point was I aware of the audience's gradual disappearance, of the emptiness that flooded the seats, because I had been *paralyzed*. The image of Elena-Marie Sandoz on the screen had *paralyzed* me and that was why I hadn't realized that all the people had silently exited the theater, leaving me alone, *paralyzed* in my seat. The municipal community theater wanted to stop showing *Eyes of Pain* that very afternoon, but

I refused to let them. I offered to pay them the full amount of thirty tickets so they wouldn't stop showing the movie. That was the full value of Elena-Marie Sandoz's image for me. The municipal community theater screened *Eyes of Pain* one more time, thanks to my having paid the full amount of thirty tickets. The appearance of Elena-Marie Sandoz on the screen was limited to thirty seconds, I counted them during the second projection of *Eyes of Pain*, and it felt natural to have paid the fee of one ticket for each second that she appeared on the screen. For those thirty seconds, Elena-Marie Sandoz was lying down, *without moving.* She wasn't dead, or asleep. For thirty seconds, Elena-Marie Sandoz looked at the viewer, looked at me without blinking once, smiling. The whole movie had been filmed in black and white, but this didn't bother me at all, as I feel that a multiplicity of colors leads to an inevitable distortion of perception. For this reason, I perceived that Elena-Marie Sandoz's black-and-white smile was directed at me in an exclusive and unrepeatable way. It couldn't be otherwise, given that I was the only one watching her at the municipal community theater during the second screening of *Eyes of Pain*. Inevitably, I would want to acquire the movie, would want no one but me to have access to her image. It felt natural to acquire *Eyes of Pain* with ease, just as it felt natural that there was *only* one copy. Since I had the *only* copy, I no longer feared it being seen by other people. Elena-Marie Sandoz's pure image belonged exclusively and entirely to me. But a *sinister thought* began to take shape in my brain. This *sinister thought* spread throughout my brain, taking up all the empty spaces, pushing at its edges, inflating it as though it were full of tainted air. Elena-Marie Sandoz was *alive*, she was a person who, with every step, every movement, every word, was causing the pure image of Elena-Marie Sandoz to deteriorate, the image that belonged to me. I obtained her information, in an *aseptic* manner, as they say, without collateral damage that would jeopardize me in the future. She lived in the city's marginal neighborhood, which was reserved for outcasts. It was a decrepit neighborhood in *very bad shape*, one that no one took care of effectively. It felt natural to see Elena-Marie Sandoz seated in a seedy bar. Her entire body was visible through the large window of the seedy bar. She was alone and slowly caressed a dirty bottle of cheap whiskey. The cheap whiskey was Elena-Marie Sandoz's only company, the only tool she had to carry out an ongoing, interminable suicide. Her body was swollen to such an extent that looking at it in its entirety was horrific. The cheap whiskey softened the perverse reality of what she had become. The decrepitude of Elena-Marie Sandoz's reality poisoned my brain, causing the *sinister thought* to push at its edges, authentically cracking my skull. Elena-Marie Sandoz's person couldn't continue to taint the image of Elena-Marie Sandoz, an image that, moreover, belonged to me. When she finished the dirty bottle of cheap whiskey, she got up and her stomach moved as though it were a live spiderweb. I disliked the repulsive way her stomach moved. In the street's artificial light, I saw that her hair was the color of a foul-smelling onion. She had on a cotton coat two sizes too big, evidencing the fact that she had stolen it or that someone had given it to her in a false act of charity. The coat was the color of rancid meat. Everything about her gave off the stench of squalor and exhaustion. The black spot that was Elena-Marie Sandoz forced me to hasten the ongoing, interminable suicide that she had embarked on, and in this way avoid the painful reality of her existence from causing the *singular* image of Elena-Marie Sandoz to deteriorate, an image that, as I have said, was my exclusive possession. On the following days, Elena-Marie Sandoz received thirty letters at the seedy bar and the boardinghouse where she slept. Their delivery was planned in a *methodical* manner to avoid damaging consequences in the future. None of the letters were signed and a *single* sentence was written on each of them, except for the last one. On the successive letters that were sent to Elena-Marie Sandoz, each sentence was repeated at random so that despite the ongoing state of disturbance that was her life, there would be no question about their *single* aim. Except for the last letter, the last one was blank. The sentences were created in a *precise* manner to achieve a *single* objective, that of hastening the ongoing, interminable suicide of Elena-Marie Sandoz. She received all of the fifteen letters sent to the seedy bar at the same time. On seeing them, she looked confused, as though she were in the presence of a serious mistake. She opened the fifteen envelopes one at a time, without reading the letters, and placed the envelopes on one side of the table and the letters in a pile on the other. She did not caress the dirty bottle of cheap whiskey, but instead looked at it insistently, ignoring the pile of fifteen letters. Her insistent gaze was accompanied by nervous breathing, and this produced a slow rolling of her stomach, which caused the spiderweb to move once again, after a period of involuntary stillness. She took two sudden sips for courage or to dissipate the mistake of having received the fifteen letters or to accept the weight of knowing that someone was aware of her corrupt existence. Elena-Marie Sandoz picked up the fifteen letters with diffi- culty, almost in pain, and read: "I'm only writing to you so I don't kill you"; "You, Elena-Marie Sandoz, must put an end to the black spot that is your life"; "No one will remember you"; "You, Elena-Marie Sandoz, tarnish the world." She didn't react right away because the cheap whiskey that had accumulated in her blood prevented her from reasoning flu- ently. But when she did, she stood up with difficulty and looked, in a *paranoid fashion*, at the people in the seedy bar, at the people in the street, and at the people in the buildings. However, she didn't see them. She was only able to look out from within the fog of alcohol, and that's why she didn't see me seated near her table. When she sat back down, she tore up each of the fifteen letters dispassionately, resigned, as though she had known all along that they had been meant for her, even if she first believed them to be a mistake. On the next day, she received fourteen letters with the same sentences written on them at random. This time she didn't open them. When she had finished drinking the cheap whiskey, she put the letters in the pocket of her coat, the one that was the color of rancid meat, and went to the boardinghouse. That was when I had the last letter delivered, the blank letter, in order to achieve the *single* aim of Elena-Marie Sandoz executing the suicide that had been ongoing and interminable. The next day, it felt natural to see a crowd gathered at the door to the boardinghouse to watch, fascinated, the body of Elena Marie-Sandoz being removed in a black plastic bag. People often stop to watch, fascinated, the minor repercussions of death in order to add a bit of fear, as it were, to the monotony of their lives. People are capable of anything to dissipate the monotony of their lives. Elena-Marie Sandoz's *singular* image belonged, as they say, exclusively to me. The infective reality that was her person no longer existed. However, a *recurrent thought* had spread though my decrepit head. Had it been her in the black plastic bag? Was it her in the Cemetery of the Silver Crosses? I needed to be absolutely sure that Elena-Marie Sandoz had *in effect* died and that she would never return to the seedy bar. The painful reality that was her person could not be allowed to cause the *singular* image of Elena-Marie Sandoz to deteriorate, an image that was, as they say, my exclusive possession. On the following days, I sat at the table she had occupied. My head was in *very bad shape* as a result of the *recurrent thought*, and it was becoming disfigured as the days passed. The *singular* image of Elena-Marie Sandoz was growing less consistent in my undesirable brain, it was coming undone in a sinister way throughout my body and my surrounds. The cheap whiskey softened the perverse reality that I was becoming. A month after the possible death of Elena-Marie Sandoz, in the seedy bar, drinking my bottle of cheap whiskey, I received fifteen letters. I took two sudden sips for courage or to dissipate the mistake of having received the fifteen letters or to accept the weight of knowing that someone was aware of my existence. The first sentence I read was: "I'm only writing to you so I don't kill you." I stood up in a *paranoid fashion* and looked at the people in the seedy bar, at the people in the street, and at the people in the buildings. However, I didn't see them. I was only able to look out from within the fog of alcohol, and that's why I didn't see myself seated at my table, the table where I undertook the execution of my interminable suicide.

# THE SLOWNESS OF PLEASURE

She's seated. Feet together, hands on a wooden bench. She's alone. Leaning back against the bench in a light knee-length skirt, a translucent shirt, her eyes silent. She's still. Her mouth half-open, breath slow, hair brushing the tips of her breasts, lips barely moving, caressing the air, vibrating subtly, like two red wings falling together, one atop the other.

People pass by but they aren't there. What's there are bodies, clothes, smells mixing with words made of nothing, of broken glass, of dead, shredded moments. There's a shortness of breath, a murmur that's dark, ridiculous, flat. Motionless, she looks at a painting.

A woman is seated in a boat made of black wood, holding a chain that imprisons her. There are reeds in the water that could slice her skin, pierce it like ice needles. There's a lantern hanging from the tip of the dark boat, and there are candles melting, burning out. There's a river, its water suspended in time, as though seeking to freeze the world, arrest it forevermore in this moment, in this perfect instant. There are tiny birds barely visible atop their perches on the reeds, on the sharp thorns penetrating the limits of the land-scape, where there is no blood.

The woman is going to die and she knows it. She's not crying. She has on a white dress, seemingly to protect her from the cold, though it doesn't. The blanket she's seated on grazes the water. It's already wet and doesn't cover her. The trees are asleep, but they hear the woman's eyes close, smell her luminous hair falling to her waist, feel her lips, the soft-ness of her fear, her mouth barely open. The cold halts the sounds, reduces them to a stillness like a cry that's distorted, mute. It wants to kill them slowly, pleasuring them. It wants the woman to disappear among the sharp caresses, shredded with a slowness possible only in death.

And she, seated, alone, still, *is* this woman, wants to be her. She needs to be in the boat, to feel the chain's frozen steel, the weight of the white dress that doesn't keep her warm. She needs to be inside the transparent and pure skin. To be this woman. Shrouded in silence, in the soft whispers of the cold enveloping her, in the motionless rhythm of the water taking her breath away. She presses her hands into the edges of the wooden bench and trembles, slightly. She's the woman seated on the embroidered blanket, she wants to be her.

She feels death, can touch its eyelids. She knows the still-ness is capable of killing her because she is now the woman inhaling the softness of the trees. She'd let herself go, fall into the endless pulse of silence.

The black boat doesn't appear to be moving, it appears trapped in the reeds, and the woman seated on the bench's light wood understands that the stillness is not death, nor is it the silence, the cold, or the woman. It's part of the landscape's breath, it's inside her just as it's in the painting, the frozen birds, the motionless reeds, the black water.

Then, keeping still, she's alone and light as she lets herself fall, her blood and veins diluting into thin threads; her mouth open, slightly; her nails digging into the wooden bench; her eyes fixed on the woman, the painting; her hair covering her wet and glistening lips, which move at a rhythm that's languid, precise, soft, like that of the black boat; all of her skin vibrating imperceptibly, almost invisibly; her breath halting for moments, like the breath of the woman who never stops dying; her legs open, her hands clutching the bench, leaving the slightest of marks in it, prizing the light wood apart. And there are no sounds, like in the painting, it's just her in a dimension at the threshold of the air's limits, where there is a single breath, and she's nearly at the precipice. Her skin is now transparent like that of the woman disappearing, spilling out of the beats pulsing with silence, beats that are born of the frozen water, the birds' stillness, the black reeds, the gaze of this woman alone. Her light skirt wrinkles over her shaking legs, she feels it doesn't cover her like the wet white dress. The birds' slight vibrations brush the hand that holds the chain, the hand clutching the bench, its nails bruising the light wood. She feels the limits of the landscape, of the world, she perceives them suspended in the air, in the reeds that are just visible, in the water with thorns, in the bench where she's seated and still.

She's not speaking, though her body seems to be, shaking with the slowness that only pleasure allows, unceasing, like on a river, in a boat.

# NO TEARS

— *For Nora Gómez* —

The first time I saw her was at Mrs. Lombardi's wake. She was dainty as a petal on a toy rose, so delicate and white in the black suit she wore, which could have been a ragdoll's, the suit of a doll at once perfect and broken. She didn't look like a woman, but like a bird, only one with no wings and no desire to fly, a bird that elicits a strange mix of compassion and repugnance. An eagle without wings. Her profile was severe, sharp, her face like Plato's, only without the brilliant aura of intelligence you'd expect. Plato without substance or personality. Sometimes I think she did have a personality, but that I couldn't see it, or that it had perhaps become diluted in the midst of the pool of stupidity expanding around her. But this was the image she wanted to give off, and it fit perfectly with her smile, the smile of a porcelain antique, a swallow dying of cold, a dainty lotus flower slowly sinking into the most repugnant of swamps. She had the eyes of a filthy, infertile, solitary cat. Her hair rained down on her face; it was pale, dirty water, water that discolors, that fissures your gaze. She was dangerous.

I first saw her standing alone next to a bouquet of calla lilies, and, before I knew she intended to challenge me and anticipated war, I was curious about her, and felt my body, and especially my skin, driven vaguely toward her, wanting to confirm the law that a fragile and delicate object can be shattered into thousands of pieces if you insert a sharp implement into it repeatedly, at a rhythm that can diminish or increase, but never, ever, cease, that in this mechanical act, precise as a clock, you can experience a kind of pain incredibly close to pleasure, only full of blood and other, less noble fluids. When I approached her and asked how she was related to the deceased, I knew she was lying, that she was a novice, a stupid bird occupying an invented space that didn't belong to her. But I thought nothing of it because I consider myself to be a good person, a peaceable one; it would be correct to say—for me to accept—that every so often someone comes along and makes another attempt, plays with the possibility of taking away the only thing that has distinguished my family, the only tradition that each of my family members has upheld without hesitation, with pride and solemnity.

My name is Juan de Tartáz. The first Tartáz to set foot on these lands in colonial times was the founder of the family legacy. José de Tartáz was his name. He spent his leisure time attending strangers' wakes. He wasn't interested in the dead person; his sole objective was to avoid tears. He couldn't bear them in any form. In the book he left behind as the comprehensive manifesto of his noble actions, *The Wake, the Family, and Tartáz*, he explains that he never shed a tear. Ever. My father, Joaquín de Tartáz, would read the Tartáz manifesto to me every night over dinner, and it was in this way that I learned the art of bringing laughter to those who can't stop crying. Logically, my father trained me to avoid tears. Mine and others'. The two of us took pride in never having cried. Ever. When he died, his last words were "Never abandon the family tradition with tears. Ever." That was his last wish.

What we do, folks, is an art form, a piece of goldsmithing, a work that, if the comparisons hold, is on par with an example I will allow myself to cite, that of Ghiberti's *Gates of Paradise*, exalted by the Baptistery of Florence. Because the work we do is of this caliber, work of a superior nature, and among the deceased's extended family we are respected and admired for its quality and for our commitment at all times. As a preliminary measure, it is necessary to ensure that the dead person's relatives don't question why a complete stranger is telling jokes at their loved one's wake. But one must also learn when it's time to begin, which is a matter of reading the atmosphere, the faces. This is followed by the choice of a suitable repertoire, because the audience members are numerous; so too are the reactions. Only once in my life, in my youth, did I have to run off under a downpour of rosaries, Bibles, and calla lilies. Of course, I couldn't have known the dead person had jumped from the ninth floor when I told the joke about the man who wanted to fly. But above all, one must learn to contain the repulsion for tears, the feeling of wanting to be sick when that transparent liquid slithers along faces, dampens clothes and food, mixes with cigarette smoke and dirty, moist handkerchiefs, slips into mouths like thousands of white worms, runs along hands, mixes with strands of hair, lingers on fingernails, devours eyes, clouds gazes, breaches the skin in its entirety, and leaves a permanent, invisible stain, a stain that grows inside one's veins, dirtying one's blood, tainting it with sadness, with death. This is perhaps the most difficult aspect of our work.

I saw the featherless eagle for the second time at Dr. Ezcurra's wake. Automatically, I chose to ignore her, to forget her presence and the winged shadow her soft little body projected, her swamp-doll body. I focused on conquering my audience, on carrying out tradition, our honorable family vocation, on sculpting smiles, chiseling them, working them like Donatello with his reliefs on the altar at Padua. I had succeeded at stopping the tears and felt it was the moment to produce smiles and ultimately laughter and applause, though never, and in this I am very careful, never hysterical laughter, because this can lead to tears. She stared at me, unblinking, as though mid-thought, as though she were truly thinking. I stopped for a second to look at her face, and I noticed, I clearly saw, that she was now a majestic eagle soaring over the room, calculating her attack. At the time, I didn't understand that her limitless fragility could hide an intelligence capable of determining the precise moment she would begin to ruin my life. But it was only a second, a minuscule fraction of time. After that she returned to her natural stance, that of a malnourished swallow.

That's why the day I saw her again, at Counselor Anchorena's wake, which took place in the afternoon, and later that evening at Mrs. Viel Temperley's, what had at first been simple curiosity and an almost metaphysical annoyance began to take the form of pure, gleaming, undivided hatred.

I saw her regarding the people with a face like a white dove's, looking like a collectible doll, but it was clear she couldn't see them. I spoke to her. "You again. Strange to encounter the same person at entirely unrelated wakes. It would appear that you're making a habit of this."

She looked at me with faded eyes full of fog and I felt the majestic eagle brush my shoulder. Immediately, I saw the liquid, the water of sadness, run down a cheek. "I came to cry and I don't like to cry alone. I don't care about whoever died, I just don't want to feel alone in my pain, and you and your stupid jokes are getting in the way. There aren't as many deaths as there should be in a place that calls itself a city. That's why I'm asking you to leave me and my wakes in peace."

The first image that came to me was of a large grave in which her little marble bones, of cracked stone, rested happily. I gently placed her white hand on mine and petted it slowly. I touched her airy skin and looked straight into her black eyes, and it was like looking into the eyes of a cat living in an abandoned lot. "If you don't leave, the last thing you'll see in life is the happy look on my face while my hands wring your hideous circus-bird neck."

Immediately, without looking at me, she burst into violent tears. Thousands of tears like transparent bees, like salty vipers, like water scorpions, like wet spiders, struck my face, my clothes, my eyes, and all I could do was run, escape, and while I did, while I searched desperately for the exit, I could see the eagle looking at me, smiling.

My options, after that tragic day, have been limited. Killing her would be the most gratifying, but tarnishing our family's honor with a murder, though entirely justified, I should clarify, would be unthinkable. Confronting her and demanding her silent retreat from my life, from my wakes, would be dangerous, unimaginable. Under no circumstances would I be able to handle another attack, another encounter with those watery eyes. Accepting defeat and disappearing, then frequenting wakes in smaller towns would be absurd, would clearly be synonymous with family betrayal and suicide, would mean brutally stomping on the Tartáz family's memory. I opted for the path of caution, for the philosophy of the hunter who simply watches and waits; who waits for the right moment to fire and then patiently picks up the eagle it has just killed with a shot between the eyes.

I saw her at Mrs. Rosales's wake. She was seated, surrounded by women who insisted on matching the rhythm of her halted breaths, drying their eyes in unison, wringing their hands as though they could cry with them. Their heads together, their black dresses forming a circle, they were so macabre and pathetic that they resembled a group of vultures, of scavengers, performing an act that was regrettable, artificial, woefully unhappy. I sat down in an armchair some distance away and waited. I did have the disproportionate and ungentlemanlike urge to go up to her, pull out a gun, and kill her on the spot with a single shot to the forehead, or with two shots, one in each eye. I was concentrating, wallowing in the image of her little face riddled with holes, her eyes full of gunpowder, when I saw her looking at me. She was surprised, her mouth slightly open, her eyebrows raised. I stared at her, penetrating the fog, the filthy, discolored sea. I looked at her for a long while, slowly, establishing my position as the hunter, turning her into the victim, into a fearful eagle, an eagle without wings. Thousands of transparent insects began to slither out of her eyes, and as she cried, she looked at me without even blinking. This was the challenge, the war, because while she carried out the farce, the deplorable representation of false pain, I could clearly make out a smile under the discolored rain. The grubby vultures mimicked the royal eagle, and when she increased the flow of tears, the rest of them tried to follow suit. They had turned the entire room into a sanctuary dedicated to pain and this was primarily her doing. However, I had to acknowledge it was a fascinating performance. They looked like black reeds swaying to the rhythm of the wind in a storm. They looked like animals, a pack of solitary dogs trembling under the frozen glints in the clouded sky. They looked like a bronze relief that was black, worn, that had a life of its own, but that was in fact dead.

I was focusing on these thoughts when I noticed the water bird looking at me. I felt her pale eyes piercing my skin, shrieking. At first I didn't understand, but then I noticed, I clearly saw, that she was looking at me in desperation. The vultures had taken the moans and tears down a notch and I understood perfectly that she had gone dry. Her eyes moved in dismay, seeking help. I knew that she saw herself repeated ad nauseam in each of these women. I knew that this was her little hell, her private torment, because now she had nothing to cry about, because she was emptier than ever before, and her wings had finally dissolved into her sadness. She needed me. She wanted me to stop the vultures, to wipe away the tears she no longer had.

I remained seated, knowing I wasn't going to do anything to help her. I looked at her without even blinking. Her little body, like that of an abandoned doll, like a toy made of mud, trembled slightly and the fog that cloaked her eyes began to dissipate. She was burning in the transparent flames of the other women's tears, sinking a little further into the swamp, into the pool of stupidity and misfortune that had begun to form under her little lotus flower shoes.

I smiled at her and, when I was ready to approach, to say into her ear that it was all over, that the time had come for her silent and definitive retreat, when I was ready to pick up my prey like a good hunter, I felt myself take flight with majestic wings over that calvary of sufferers, felt her to be a mouse in the mud, dying of cold, on the brink of madness. My flight was full, absolute, because it contained everything, including her, and this resulted in a pleasure that had no form because it encompassed all forms, nor were there words for it, because all words were inside it. For that reason, I've never understood why it was then, right during my solemn flight as a royal eagle, that a tear, a goddamn water bug, the abhorrent sign of familial failure, gently rolled out of my left eye.

# THE CONTINUOUS EQUALITY OF THE CIRCUMFERENCE

A circle. This is what Ada wants to be. She's not interested in holding abstract ideas in her head. She wants to be a circle. Not to imagine herself as an unreal, hypothetical circle. She wants to form one. She needs her body to take on the round, infinite shape of a circle. All my extremities should converge in a single point, she thinks. She jots this down on a piece of paper. Not just any piece of paper, taken randomly from a notebook, but one she has cut the edges off. A circle of paper.

She understands that, by definition, a circle is flat. She knows that to transform herself into a circle that has volume, into a live sphere, would be an unparalleled feat. And yet she considers the use of the word *sphere* to define herself unacceptable. She distrusts the harsh sound it emits when she thinks it, when she writes it. The sound halts her, disturbs her. She discards the word *sphere*. She spits it out, tosses it aside, forgets it. She adopts the word *circle*, because this is what she wants to be.

She conceives of a plan, a plan that will convert her skin into the circumference of a circle. She prepares to embody, in flesh and bone, the assertion that the circle is the most perfect of geometrical shapes. Because that's what Ada wants to be: beautiful, eternal, perfect. She wants to be the divine abode in which the sacred is housed.

Saint Augustine said it, and she has always venerated the saints: "Most beautiful is the circle, which has no angles to disrupt the continuous equality of its circumference. Above all of these, however, is the point—indivisible, center and beginning and end of itself, the generating point of the circle, the most beautiful of all the figures."

Ada doesn't need to reread Saint Augustine's words or even to write them down. She repeats them every morning and night like someone repeating an endless prayer that always returns to where it began. Through her thoughts and actions, she wants to put an end to her despicable reality and balance it with a truth that's mathematical, dense, unbreakable. A compelling truth. She wants to purge what is provisional and indefinite in search of what is lasting, what constitutes certainty, plenitude. To ensure her circular body is the only refuge.

Outside the secure space of the circle, vulgarity accumulates. Ada loathes vulgarity because it's there that misery hides. She knows that misery is destructive and, as such, ephemeral.

Animals, things, and people—she finds them all difficult to bear. They seem like prosaic, lackluster entities. She tolerates them because she intuits they won't disappear, at least not for the time being. Someday, perhaps, they'll all vanish, all the irregular shapes will disappear forever and at the same time. Except for her. She'll remain because of her circularity, thanks to which she'll be inextinguishable.

How can one be a circle? she asks herself. A circle doesn't have extremities, she concludes. So she outlines a plan to cut off her arms and legs. But my head is an extremity that will prevent my body from being a perfect circle, she reasons. It would be stupid to cut off my head because then I'd be a dead circle, and that doesn't interest me. She decides she can live with being two circles. Better still, she figures, as that would be double the perfection.

She observes her body. Before cutting off her extremities, she has to gain weight. It's embarrassing to be a big rectangle. I'm a deformed rectangle, she yells. She needs to find a way to blow herself up, to take on the shape of a balloon. Her skin needs to stretch until she's a big ball of flesh and fat. She imagines herself as a rosy disk and is pleased.

She chooses a precise diet to achieve her goal. Despairing somewhat, she realizes that gaining weight is just as difficult as losing it, if not more. She doesn't understand. Her body retains the inexact shape of a rectangular plank. She decides that movement is preventing her from achieving her goal. If I move I burn fat, she reflects. And this is stopping me from carrying out my task. She reaches the conclusion that the couch is a good spot to transform into a circle, and to control her body's evolution, she orients the mirror in such a way as to see all of herself reflected in it.

Seated and furious, she notices that her body remains a quadrangular beam. She's flat, ridiculous and flat, an erroneous combination she cannot accept. In addition to complete rest, she resolves to change her diet and eat round foods. Out of sympathy, their shape will affect my internal structure, and this will help me become a circle, she speculates. She decides she shouldn't chew these foods, so they don't lose their essential purity.

She sits down on the couch surrounded by plates of grapes, small plums, and ball-shaped candies and cookies. She scarfs these down. For a second, she feels she's going to choke, but she relaxes and a plum descends intact through her digestive system.

Ada perceives her body taking on the sublime shape of a balloon and congratulates herself.

She decides the time has come to cut off her legs and then her arms, useless annexes that hinder her final objective. After she has conducted initial research on anatomy and devised a system of pulleys and sharp strings to sever her legs and arms without assistance, she decides to do so. Perfection has its price, she confirms. Despite the pain and the blood, Ada is pleased.

She immediately realizes a fundamental fact. Without her extremities, she won't be able to feed herself and will lose her circular shape.

Ada observes the abyss that the couch has become and decides to jump. There's no such thing as sacrifice when you want to be inextinguishable, she repeats, landing on the plate of grapes. The plate breaks under the weight of her body and the shards pierce the skin of the living circumference that is Ada.

Despite the pain and the blood, she detects the cookies nearby. The grapes no longer fulfill the fundamental require-ment of being round because they are now a soft and shapeless mass, and as such, useless. She rolls along the floor toward the food, but her right arm, lying there inert, blocks the way. Ada tries to push it, but the circularity of her body forces her to return, inevitably, to where she started. She decides to try the other direction and discovers a cookie very close to one of her legs. The cookie is in a pool of blood, but it has retained its annular shape, so Ada resolves to eat it. She ignores the pieces of glass that sink into her skin and rolls in the opposite direction. My pain is also circular, she thinks, and smiles. She rotates until she feels an obstacle. It's her left arm and it prevents her from moving forward.

While she plans how to navigate around the arm, she notices an intact grape very close to her mouth. She sticks out her tongue and devours it. The grape gets stuck in Ada's throat and, as she chokes, she thinks that it's all in vain. The mirror is too far for her to admire the perfection she has become.

117

# A HOLE HIDES A HOUSE

There is an hour of the afternoon when the plain is on the verge of saying something. It never says it, or perhaps it says it infinitely, or perhaps we do not understand it, or we understand it and it is as untranslatable as music.

—Jorge Luis Borges

The woman boils the water and stokes the fire. It's hot inside. She needs to have everything ready before the master, who's off in the woods, is back. Today is her last day of work for this man. He's going to pay her the pittance she's earned for two days of labor. She's not doing it for the money, but for the girl in the room. The master took the girl away from her father and now he keeps her as his lover and cook, his spouse and child, his prostitute and washerwoman. She's fifteen years old.

The woman doesn't know her name. The master said, "Attend to the girl," and then left. The only thing the girl does is lie in bed and look through the hole in the roof of her room. Her condition is no longer serious, but she was close to death yesterday. The woman sits down and swallows a piece of dry

**119**

bread. Now she has to cook the stew, sweep the dirt, and knead the bread. She has to feed the animals, clean the clothes, and put the yerba maté out to dry in the sun.

She looks through the garbage for some paper or a piece of cardboard to cover the hole. Every time she goes into the girl's room, she feels the dry cold on her back. It's not right for a sick girl to convalesce in a room with a broken roof that lets in insects and the icy wind, which is rare at this time of year. She finds nothing, not even a piece of cloth.

The girl lost a lot of blood yesterday. The woman has just dressed her wounds and brought her soup. The hole seemed bigger, darker. And now it's late, and there's no time to fix the roof. She can't even cover the hole with dry leaves. The master will be back soon and she has to have everything ready.

It's a big room, with no windows. The girl hears the woman that the master hired sweep the dirt floor. She looks up at the hole in the roof. She barely moves, barely breathes. The sky she sees is blue, green, at times white. It's just a hole that hides a house. It's just a house that, little by little, or all of a sudden, will fall to pieces. There are no dry reeds covering the hole geometrically, infinitely. There isn't even a blanket over it, or a piece of paper. The master told her she would have to get used to the hole, that he couldn't be expected to take care of such things. It doesn't rain around here at this time of year, he said, and the day the clouds cry out, he'd move the bed off to the side, and she'd lie there, watching the room flood.

She stretches the old sheets and if she's cold it's because her uterus is empty, full of air. The master forced her to kill the baby that had been in there, where now she feels the cold. Just like he forced her to abort the baby that would have been born in March, and the one conceived in February of some other year.

The girl lights a cigarette and the smoke clings to the walls. The master doesn't know she smokes, doesn't know the smoke is mixing with the cold. Now she can smell the meat the woman is boiling and hear her chopping vegetables. Insects enter through the hole. Spiders and mosquitoes invade the room. The woman tried to kill them, tried to cover up the hole, but she couldn't.

There's a large knife under the girl's pillow. She stole it two months ago from the farmhand who works on the ranch next door. She'd gone over to sell some eggs, and when the man went to look for a basket to place them in, he left the knife unguarded on the table. She doesn't know why she did it. She simply picked the knife up, ran her fingers over its blade, and hid it under some bread and fried pastries.

The woman is filling the bowls with chicken feed. She'll be leaving soon and the girl will have to take care of the rest.

Someone enters the house. The girl knows it's the master because of the smell of horses and sweat. She puts out the cigarette, hides it. Pretends to be asleep. The master won't even give her a day of rest. He's going to force her to work, to lie down in his bed, to take care of the house and the animals, because that's what he's done in the past. Things aren't going to be any different now that she's older and in pain.

He enters the room. She trembles. Squeezes her eyes shut. The hole seems bigger, darker.

"It's time to get up. Let's go."

She's unable to speak, all she wants is to escape through the hole.

"Get up, damn it! I've paid the woman. You take care of the rest."

"It hurts."

"Get up or I'll whip you to death."

The girl runs her fingers over the knife. She looks at the hole and feels cold. Slowly, she rises, supporting herself on the wall. She sits up and breathes. She looks the master in the eye like she's pleading with him, but he goes up to her, the whip in his hand, and he doesn't stop looking at her as though he wants to penetrate her, empty her, kill her.

She stops looking at him. She wants to sleep, to get warm. He has the whip raised over her head, and as she sees the hole get smaller, she runs her fingers over the knife again and stabs him quickly. She kills his dead heart and slices out his cries with a cut to the throat. He's sprawled on the floor and she sees the hole get bigger, sees a piece of the roof fall onto the bed. She takes off his bloodied shirt and tries to cover the hole, but the roof is rotten and falls to pieces.

The sky floods her, she feels it's white, green, at times black. The hole covers her up. There are no reeds or shirts capable of blocking it. No paper or blankets. She wants to scream, but no longer has the strength. She squeezes her eyes shut and falls.

The sky is green, blue, at times red.

# HELL

A constellation burns inside the stone.

—Marosa di Giorgio

Three old women are walking together. Arm in arm, they weave a symbiosis outside of time. Their bones, which cradle the precariousness of their bodies, are mineralized under their skin. The liquid in their veins is embroidered, the pearl lacework forming designs that link them in their weariness. They love one another because they repulse one another.

The women levitate, heavy in the trilogy that nurtures them. They appear motionless, their starched blood delaying all action, but they walk on, so slowly it's absurd.

The seconds that immortalize them come apart in the silence of the burning morning.

They're carrying a bird in a cage. The creature's swollen flesh defies the solid black bars. Inert, it contemplates the old women, their pallid sway. They pet the tender tips of its feathers. This contact is silky, obscene, and the bird wishes it could cry out from within the stillness.

Undaunted, the old women maneuver their instability, covering the ground to the park. They form a compact wall of unbreakable fragility. They continue, refreshed, rapacious, translucent. Their breath weaves invisible threads, uniting them in the daily tedium brought about by affection that's repetitive, futile, fragmentary. In unison, they take a seat, perform an incomprehensible and archaic dance. They unfurl feigned aromas and wrinkles and rancid ruffles that combine and expand in vain.

The minutes that sustain them come apart in the thick air of the inflamed day.

Ceremoniously, they put the cage down. It strikes the stone ground, and the vibrations spoil the creature's apathy. The stone is hot; it's boiling, burning. The creature tries to move its body and the cage shifts slightly. A feather falls, then another. The old women give one another looks of dignified dismay, and, docilely, they secure the cage with shoes that wound the dry flesh and tense talons. The bird cowers in the cage, it wants to shrink to the edges of inexistence. The old women pet it and their love is merciless, authentic.

They take out a bag of bread. It crinkles, drawing doves and swallows. Crystalline smiles form on the women's faces as they toss the bread with exasperating levity. The bird convulses at the impossibility, the aberration. They ignore it, ecstatic before the predatory multitude, though they don't stop compressing the cage, crushing the creature's body, sullying its white feathers with the filth of their pointy low heels.

The hours that edify them break apart in the blazing light.

The hot stone alters the doves' and swallows' senses. It dazes them, but they don't stop eating. An imperceptible violence slips between the wings, the beaks, and the claws. A dove attacks a swallow. Kills it. Blood boils on stone. The old women waver inside their panic. Unable to stand, they sit suspended in the incomprehension of shattered equilibrium. They look at the dead swallow, their mouths stunned, lacquered, cracked.

The days that mold them burst open in the charred afternoon.

The bird feels the cage decompress. The shoes have stopped tormenting it and now it can move its wings. It flails around the cage; the heat from the stone clings to the black bars and burns its skin. The cage convulses and overturns. A smothering, hollow sound is heard—the bird's left wing breaking into three. Then a precise, metallic sound—a screw loosening. The bird feels no pain because the door opens with a sacred slowness. The old women don't notice it, alert as they are to the dead swallow, to the red liquid frothing on the ground.

The creature pokes its head out the door. It feels the seconds, minutes, hours, and days in pieces that fall onto its white feathers. It trembles slightly. The old women see it, pick up the cage, crush it against the hot bars, and close the door.

Irrationally, the bird knows, comprehends, that of the possible constellations, in all the possible universes, this is the first glimpse of hell.

A feather falls, then another.

# ARCHITECTURE

— *For Rubén González* —

The stained glass isn't authentic. The originals were destroyed by the Normans and had to be replaced with glass that was painted. Logically, they chose the figure of Christ His Majesty for the central pane, Christ being the most important figure, the cornerstone of the Catholic edifice. He's surrounded by four silhouettes: a lion, an eagle, an ox, and a man. They represent the germ of the church, the foundation of the Great Christian Empire. They're looking at Christ with devotion, but he's busy holding up a sealed book, seated on the emperor's throne, the King of Kings's throne, exalted in a cruciform halo, looking at nothing, at infinity, probably at the real God. He doesn't even sense the group of small bodies camouflaged against the dark oak of the bench, the black shadows in which the shape of a bony structure can barely be made out, the deformed group that is now an integral part of the architecture.

The words of these faded spirits shape the space. They stop at the central apse, slowly cracking the altar's marble columns; they cover the cupola's mosaics, stripping them of color, sinking into the Virgin Mary's blue blanket as she screams inconsolably before a crucified Christ; they circle the white eyes of Saint Prudence, brush the open mouth full of pain, the painted tears, the red heart that's torn apart and strives to beat in her hands; they drag themselves along the frozen floor covered in marble slabs that are worn by the weight of so many sins contained in a single place.

The air may appear luminous to the purest of them. All want to position themselves next to the apse, the altar, which was built facing east because it is in this cardinal point that the sun breathes, that its rays slip violently through the windows, illuminating the sacred altar with sweet, false, and ecclesiastical colors. All want to be flooded in that celestial light, to bathe in the platonic irradiation, to ascend to the white heavens.

The space may also appear somber to those who are not yet worthy of the divine splendor. The gloom reproduces, copulates in the lateral naves, the confessionals, the crypts underground. The air is cooler there, the sculptures of the saints less holy, the souls as sinful as the darkness that taints them.

The confessionals are made of carved wood with little miniatures that represent the Holy Family's flight into Egypt. They're useless. Four pieces of wood united by guilt, varnished with the sweet sensation of power the confessor cultivates.

In the septentrional nave's south confessional—an insertion between the construction's weak pillars that supports the weight of cross vaults like nerves, like veins bulging out of the church's skin—in this confessional there grows a bleak and heavy hum that rasps at the young wood. This hum is a cluster of imperfect words with a particular, distinct motion. A cluster of black stones suspended in the air. That which is sharp and dark damages the marble, weakens the pillars.

A swarm of prayers creeps out of the confessionals and down from the benches. The church is an enormous vessel of words like shouts, full of pieces of souls, of time, of empty crystals. The words are held in the air like opaque lights, waiting for immaculate absolution. Millions of them are compressed in the space, moving slowly like a great insect, seeking the redemptive gaze of Christ His Majesty.

They confront him.

This black dragonfly, this great insect of words, looks him in the eye, but the savior is absorbed in holding up the Book with Seven Seals, alert to the gaze of his church's fathers, conscious of the importance of the throne on which he's worshipped, admired by the infinite martyrs who died in his honor, weary of the words.

The insect shudders in pain. The tremor is negligible, a tiny drop falling slowly into flames. But the movement produces an acute absence. The space is perfect, the light broken. The dragonfly of the night vibrates and engenders a violent void that settles into the walls, the architecture. It's a great spiderweb of transparent threads that destroys the celestial breath.

The silence can't absorb the words and kill the black insect—it's so sharp, the silence begins to bleed. Silent red tears strike the stained glass, giving rise to a slight, almost nonexistent tremor.

The specters that are barely breathing, that hold their rosaries as though they were the last veins in their bodies, these numb mortal remains don't see what's happening, they think this structure contains the way out, the gratification, the pardon for existing. They don't feel the great black dragonfly brush their bowed heads with its legs. They can't touch the fear of silence that grows distant, seeks to disappear. The empty music the specters emit, the small black insects they spit out, these merge with the dark dragonfly in an imperceptible dance. Slowly, they destroy the building at a gentle, weary pace. These words that seek salvation are enclosed in the frozen space, in the static block crowned by Christ His Majesty, by Christ the Emperor, from which no one, not even God, can escape.

# MARY CARMINUM

She told me we were going to see a rock band, and I put on a leather jacket. I'm not exactly sure why, maybe to fit in with something. And even though it was hot, I kept the jacket on. It had studs on it and smelled a little musty because I didn't wear it often.

Before I got into the car I lit a cigarette and called El Flaco.

"Hey, Flaco, have you picked yours up?"

"I'm on it."

"Looks like we're going to see a band."

"Did yours tell you which one?"

"No."

"Neither did mine. I asked her, but she said it was a surprise. See you there, wherever it is they're taking us."

"Okay. We'll see if you catch up to me, Flaco."

"The last couple were solid nines, I'm thinking I've been ahead of you for a while now."

"Solid nines? The last one was more like a seven and that's pushing it. And you cheated, you used the old pill to knock her out."

"There's no proof. I'm appealing that judgment."

"You'll have to take that to the president."

"The president . . . right. Don't make me laugh. Today you become ex-champion."

"Don't be late, Flaco."

I stopped by her place to pick her up. When she got into the car, I saw she was wearing a long dress under a light coat. The dress was blue, bright blue. She'd done her hair in curls that fell artificially onto her shoulders, and an appliquéd blue flower held an impossibly intricate bun. She was heavily made up. Because of the whole outfit, she seemed older than she was. I looked at her in silence, unsure how to say that her clothing was absurd, outdated. When she moved in to kiss me on the cheek I heard her dress rustle. I was hot, but I wasn't going to take off my jacket, because under it I had on a Black Sabbath T-shirt.

"Why are you wearing a long dress if we're going to see a rock band?"

She looked at me, a bit surprised. "You don't like my dress?"

To avoid answering, I opened the window. Then I closed it and put on the air-conditioning. I smelled roses. The scent was dense, saccharine. "That rose smell—is that something you're wearing?"

"Yes, it's my perfume. I love it. What do you think?"

I didn't answer. The smell was oppressive, she was wearing the kind of cologne that's sold at the supermarket. I opened the window and started the engine. Then I turned it off. This wasn't going to work. I lowered my head in defeat; I knew there was no way I'd win the bet. El Flaco was going to earn points on this one, because even though she was almost an eight, with her clothes and hair and that makeup, she was a six, max. I was thinking I'd come up with some excuse to cancel, say I wasn't feeling well, but she touched my arm kind of timidly and said, "Let's go." There was an unexpected violence in her voice that silenced me. A six is better than nothing, I thought, and even though El Flaco is catching up, he's not close enough to win. He says his is an eight point five but he always exaggerates. She's gotta be a five.

"Where are we going?" I asked her.

She settled into the seat and the fabric of her dress gave off a sound like an animal slithering.

"To Fátima's neighborhood, have you been there? It's not far."

It seemed strange that there was a venue or bar in that neighborhood. I knew it was very quiet.

"There's a band playing in Fátima's neighborhood?"

"Yes."

It was a curt reply, but she smiled at me and her eyes seemed cold.

When we reached our destination I asked her if this was really where we were going, and she said yes, we were there.

I thought it might be a clandestine party and was intrigued. We were at a simple house, you might even say it was run-down. The front door was made of sheet metal and there was only one window. She didn't ring the bell; she just opened the door and went in. I'm not sure why, but I looked at her feet then, and saw she had on low heels made of something artificial and sparkly. She let me in and raised her right foot a little to show me her shoe. "Do you like them?"

El Flaco and I also take clothes into consideration, we know a great deal about the subject, and those shoes were twenty or thirty years old. You could see the glue used to stick on the plastic diamonds. Threads hung from the hem of her dress as though it had been sewn in a rush. I looked at her left shoe. One of the diamonds was missing and the soles of both feet were worn. "Yeah, they're great."

She smiled at me and said, "Come on in."

It was a small room. There was a table and chair made of pinewood. On the table I saw a plaster figurine that hadn't been painted, and guessed it was a saint. It was far too big for the table, which looked rickety. I managed to ask, "A rock band, playing here?" But she took my hand without answering and led me to another door, also made of sheet metal. She opened it and we walked down a flight of stairs, then through a long and dark hallway. I smelled something sickeningly sweet and acrid. It reminded me of the liquid that pools at the bottom of a garbage bin. I let go of her hand to cover my nose and realized she'd gotten something sticky on it.

We continued to walk through the hallway. I hadn't imagined this run-down house would be so big. We came to another door, a sturdy one this time, it might have even been armored. Over the lintel, there was a very bright lightbulb. She knocked on the door in a strange way. After two quick knocks, she let a second go by, then struck the door again. She repeated this three times while moving her lips. I noticed a drop of sweat slip from her temple to the edge of her jaw. She had on a base of pressed powder so thick that the drop left a mark, a fissure.

The door opened slowly, as though something heavy were being moved. She took my hand again, forcefully, and we stepped into a huge room with tables and chairs and a stage. I let go of her hand because it was sticky, as well as sweaty. Without her seeing me I looked for a napkin on the tables, but couldn't find one. I tried to wipe my hand on one of the tablecloths, but the sticky substance wouldn't come off. There were about fifty people there, all dressed for a party. I felt out of place in my Black Sabbath shirt and leather jacket. I kept the jacket on because it was cold, though I couldn't understand why since there were no windows. We sat down at a table close to the stage. But then she stood up and started exchanging friendly greetings with the people she knew. These people looked at me but didn't say anything. Some of them blatantly pointed at me and then hugged her. A woman wearing a crown came over to the group. The woman hugged her, removed the flower appliqué, and placed the crown on her head. The crown had stars on it. She was moved, and her bun came undone. Her curly hair looked better loose. Half point in her favor. Six point five. The little princess wearing her crown and shoes with their fake diamonds, I thought, and felt a bit of contempt. I looked at the group carefully. It was all women. They wore long skirts in different shades of blue. Navy blue, light blue, cerulean, cobalt, indigo. I didn't know what was going on. I thought of a secret costume party. I went to wipe my hand on a tablecloth, but before I did, I realized it was covered in the sticky substance. I don't know why I hadn't noticed this before.

I stood up and walked over to a table decorated with flowers. The flowers were fabric roses—white, golden, pink. They looked dirty. There were crustless sandwiches on the tables, but the bread was stale, the edges curled. On white paper plates there were mini pastries shaped like hearts. More food picks than necessary were placed next to each. These were shaped like daggers. I counted them because I found this disturbing. There were seven food picks per heart. I reached for a french fry from a plate and took a bite, but it was damp, and I spat the piece into my hand and left it on the table. Now there was grease from the fry on my hand as well as the sticky substance. There was nothing to drink and I began to feel hot again. I wanted to get out of there.

I looked around for El Flaco, but couldn't see him. The room was too big. It was a sea of blue dresses. I picked up my phone to send him a message, but there was no reception. El Flaco's always wanting to get ahead of me. No doubt he's made a pit stop at a no-tell motel, I thought. I bet he plans to throw it in my face later, wanting more points for the speed with which he achieved his goal. But without proof, without photos, he's got nothing. I'm still beating him. I felt a little better then.

I walked around the tables. The floor was filthy, the soles of my shoes stuck to it. While I looked for the bathroom to wash my hands, I noticed there were almost no men. I counted three. They weren't talking, and were seated at different tables, alone. I looked at the women closely. They all seemed worn out, as though the excessive makeup and curled hair were an attempt at hiding premature old age. They smiled a lot and some of them were so pale they looked sickly, something their makeup didn't conceal.

I couldn't find a bathroom.

The lights were turned on and off. The woman I was there with distanced herself from the group to come find me. She motioned to me to sit down. I walked over to the table slowly, still unable to process my thoughts. It was insane to think that this proud and inordinately happy woman, wearing a starry crown and shoes with plastic diamonds on them, would join me at a motel that night. Clearly, I wasn't going to win. Besides, I didn't want El Flaco to have to deal with this madness. As soon as I saw him we'd take off running. We'd cancel the competition. Though, knowing him, he'd for sure end up drunk and dancing with the crown on his head, hugging all the women in blue.

When I sat down we were served a brown drink that was like Coke, only it was warm and had no fizz. Of course they didn't serve alcohol. Flaco, we need to get ourselves out of here, I thought. The woman was sitting up straight and smiling. She seemed very happy. The other women came over to greet her, and they congratulated her as though she'd done something amazing. I took out a cigarette, but before I could light it another woman came over and lowered my hand gently, shaking her head. She was smiling so much that I could see her teeth were stained yellow with a bit of brown. Her lips had no flesh to them, they were thin and white. Her dress was made of a shiny material and when she moved it gave off a sound like that of something crawling. I smelled the roses, the same cheap and strong cologne. I also smelled her breath. There was something rotting in that lipless mouth. She had eyes like a fish or a reptile, her hair was dry and dull as though she lacked nutrients. There were tiny lines in her face where the tension in her skin seemed to have cracked her foundation. Slowly, I put the cigarette in the pack, and then put the pack away, without taking my eyes off her teeth. When she left, I tried to wipe my hand clean again. The sticky substance was black and I couldn't get it off. I asked her where the bathroom was, but she motioned to me to be quiet.

I went about observing the men. They were dressed in black trousers and white shirts. They were pale and stared at fixed points. No one was talking to them. The place was very well lit, and the walls were completely white, though there were damp stains on them. They'd tried to cover these up with garlands, some of which had come unstuck at one end and were hanging by the other. There were no instruments on the stage. She told me the show was about to begin and laughed in a way that seemed a little like choking. She was very excited and moved about in her seat.

The lights were turned off.

Six young women and one older woman appeared onstage. All wore long, identical blue dresses. The dresses were too big, as though the women had gotten their sizes wrong. Each woman had very long, straight hair that fell to her waist. Including the older woman. I was surprised an older woman would let her gray hair grow so long. The dresses had flower appliqués on them but some of the flowers seemed to have come unsewn and were about to fall off. They wore plastic pearl necklaces and matching earrings. One of them held an electric guitar that was unplugged.

I understood this was the rock band. I laughed and she glared at me. In the half-light of the room, I could see she was smiling at me, only it was with rage. I averted my gaze and heard one of the men near our table begin to clap softly, as though in slow motion. A woman lowered his arms.

The band unrolled a sign with large, shiny letters on it that read "Mary Carminum." The audience began to clap. The man near our table stared at the floor. A thread of drool fell from his mouth. A woman next to him took his hands and moved them, imitating applause. The woman who had brought me

141

put her face to my ear and said, "They're Mary's songs." I looked at her without understanding. She added, "Mary, the mother of Christ, the mother of humanity, the mother that unites us, that loves us. We sing to her." I thought I heard the fabric of her dress swishing. It was hot, but I zipped up my jacket. Where was El Flaco?

Techno music began to play, with a lot of amp. The band onstage barely moved, though they took little steps forward and backward. The older woman went about putting gold paper crowns on each of the singers. It was then that all the women in the audience took out their paper crowns and put them on, except for mine, who was already wearing the original crown. She adjusted it and sat up straight. Her eyes sparkled.

One of the women onstage went up to the microphone and began to sing. She was out of tune. They were all out of tune. They moved their hands, tried to act, to represent what they were singing. It looked like they were moving invisible threads on the stage. They sang verses that rhymed, like "Mary, you're my dream, you're my fantasy, you spout from the very heart of me," and "Mary, my goddess, my soul, fill me whole, with your energy, mother Mary." The woman on guitar pretended to be playing, but she didn't hit a single note. The women in the audience danced in their seats and clapped. I got a better look at them and saw that they'd all hung wooden crucifixes around their necks. They were raising them and kissing them. The men also had on crucifixes. One

142

of them appeared to be partnered with a woman who took his hands and moved them, trying to get him to dance. The other two clapped very slowly, while staring at nothing. Casually, I covered my mouth with my hands so no one would see I was laughing uncontrollably. It's that I didn't know what I was doing there, everything was so absurd. I tried to breathe deeply, to calm myself down, but the woman smiled at me. She held my gaze as though she could wound me with her eyes. The band was now performing something that resembled rap. She stood up, reached for a wooden crucifix on a table, and put it on me. As she did, I got up suddenly and knocked the chair over. The women stopped singing. The music was turned off and someone flicked the lights back on. I looked around for the exit, then took the crucifix off and threw it to the floor. I heard stifled shouts. Very slowly and very clearly, someone said, "You don't do this to Mary's son." The women stood up, looked at me silently, and began to walk. They came toward me as they put blindfolds over their eyes.

I ran to the exit. The door was blocked by a white sculpture that might have been marble. I tried to move it, but it was too heavy. The sculpture was of a woman with her hands outstretched, as though in offering, and her mouth open like she was pleading. A rosary had been placed in one of her hands and in the other I made out a black mark. She was blindfolded, and blood or fresh red paint was trickling down from her eyes to her jaw. I thought I saw something move behind the gauze that covered them. When I tried to take off the blindfold, I was struck in the back of the head and lost consciousness. The last thing I heard was the swishing of the dresses approaching.

When I woke, I was confused. I didn't know where I was and my head was throbbing. Just opening my eyes was a struggle. I was nauseated, my mouth was dry, and I couldn't focus my eyes. I felt dazed. Then someone gave me a drink and I felt better. After a while, I began to remember everything that had happened and I tried to scream. I tried to get up, but I couldn't move. I no longer felt the weight of my jacket on my shoulders, or the light fabric of my T-shirt. When I was able to open my eyes and focus them, I saw I was wearing a white shirt and different trousers. They'd taken off my jeans. I thought I could make out the woman who'd brought me approach and give me little pats on the hand, which was still dirty. She smiled at me, calmly and violently. I smelled the roses again and heaved. The band was still singing, but I couldn't understand the lyrics. I saw a thread of drool fall onto my trousers.

I don't know how much time passed, but when I was starting to feel a bit better, someone hugged me and shook me. I heard El Flaco's voice. He was talking quickly, he was excited, it was clear he'd just arrived, that he didn't know what was going on. He laughed, shook me again, and said, "Wait till you see the photos. What is this place? Are you that drunk? Everything okay? You're looking pale, champ." But before I could even glance at him, a woman wearing a crown, the real one, led him to another table. While he walked away, I thought I saw him try to wipe his hand on a tablecloth.

The members of Mary Carminum were still singing.

\*       \*       \*

Hours have passed, maybe it's been days. They hung another crucifix around my neck. I've gone over what happened again and again, trying to make sense of it in my mind. I need to understand if it's real. I see El Flaco at another table. He's wearing a white shirt, like mine. My head has stopped throbbing, I'm no longer nauseated, but I can't stand up or speak. I don't know what they did to me. The woman that brought me here gives me her eternal, unhinged smile. She's wearing a paper crown and her makeup is running. Now they're singing about Mary and the miracle of the roses. I think I'm in the mood to clap.

# THE SOLITARY ONES

You walk quickly because you know the last train is leaving in less than fifteen minutes. You asked the man at the ticket stand when you took the subway in the morning. You did this because you suspected your boss would make you stay late, that he wouldn't care it was December 31, or about the parties and the toasts. "It's because the electricity was out, we have to make up for lost time," he told you, but you intuited that he actually couldn't stand his wife and kids, and so would rather be at work.

The downtown streets are empty. You're alone. You think about a movie you saw where the single people were taken to a hotel. They were forced to find a partner in forty-five days or they were turned into animals. At the hotel, the people were shown the benefits of being with a partner. One of these was that women accompanied by a man were less likely to be raped. You walk faster still and are enraged at being a cliché: the young

147

woman alone and afraid as she walks along a deserted street. You slow down and distract yourself by thinking what animal you'd like to be. An eagle. Then you look at the time and pick up your pace. You're going to miss the last train. You try to run, but your feet hurt. You walk resolutely and the sound of your heels on the pavement echoes throughout the block.

You reach Plaza de Mayo. It's deserted. People are sitting down to eat, you think. Your family is serving themselves dinner, concealing their annoyance, because you're late, yet again. You'd told them there would be no taxis since the drivers don't return to work until after one in the morning, and there was an accusatory silence from your mother, and all you managed to say was that taxi drivers celebrate New Year's too, and that you couldn't do anything about this, nor did you want to. "I'll get the last train, Mamá. I'll be there on time."

At the entrance to Line A you feel you've been struck by a dense smell. The smell is familiar, and yet it never ceases to surprise you. You always describe it as the smell of a dead dog rotting in the sun. This is Line A's characteristic smell, even at night. You take the stairs quickly but carefully, because of your heels. You see a train at the platform and know it's the last one of the night. As you press your subway pass to the turnstile, you hear the operator blow his whistle to announce that the train is leaving. You run and make it into the last car right as the doors are closing.

You sit down and breathe. When you take out your phone you see three missed calls from your mother. There's no reception so you can't call her back. Since the battery is almost dead, you turn the phone off, put it away, and look around the car. It's empty. What you feel is relief and a certain happiness at riding—for the first time, you think—in a car that's completely empty. You can't believe your luck when you remember what it was like yesterday morning. The station was full of people—the result of the subway being delayed due to the electricity outages. Your right cheekbone was plastered against the glass door and you felt that your lungs were on the verge of collapse. The skin of several sweaty people was pressed against your recently ironed shirt. A woman, whose breath smelled of coffee, cigarettes, and garlic, and whose face was five centimeters from yours, said, "Sorry, dear, you know what it's like, every morning the same thing, it's hell," and all you wanted was for her to close her mouth, but you smiled because this woman was preferable to the furious tears of the baby behind you and the two passengers who were arguing and shouting at each other because one of them had elbowed the other in the ribs.

You breathe with relief because you're alone, because the air-conditioning is on, because of the artificial scent of lemon. You lean out and look into the next car. The entire train must be empty, you figure, and imagine taking off your shoes and running from one end to the other, the train in motion, and feeling something like freedom. It would be inappropriate, you think. Your mother uses the word *inappropriate* to describe anything she doesn't approve of. The year has almost come to an end and you consider yourself deserving of an inappropriate act to greet the new one. You're about to take off a shoe when the train reaches Lima Station and a man gets on. You're paralyzed by the rancid and rotten smell that fills the car. Instinctively, you cover your nose and see the man take a seat in front of you. He's wearing a black suit that's too big. It's old and ripped. He looks at you and you're surprised by the intensity of his gaze. You assume, because of the smell of wine, that he must be drunk, and drunks usually have turbid, unhinged gazes. He looks at you like he knows something. You consider the possibility of changing cars. Though you don't want to be rude, you can't handle the smell and the way he's looking at you. He leans forward and you don't know if he's going to be sick or attack you. You go tense. But then he stands up and says, "They're waiting for you." The train reaches Sáenz Peña Station and he gets off. You don't have time to ask who "they" are and where and why they're waiting for you. You think that "they" are your family and that they are indeed waiting for you, and you calm down. You'll be there just in time for the toast.

The train passes Congreso Station. The half stations are next, you think, the incomplete ones, the solitary ones. Pasco and Alberti have always irritated you because they only go in one direction, because they've been severed. You know, because you read it, that these stations had their pairs and that they were closed down. Every time you pass them, this saddens you. You ask yourself which animal each station would choose. You imagine Pasco being a small mouse and Alberti a lizard sunning itself. You turn on your phone and try to call your mother. There's no reception. You walk to the next car to see if there's reception there. But then the electricity cuts out and the train stops.

The darkness is complete. "The electricity is out again in this goddamn city," you say under your breath. You feel around with your hands for the seats and decide to sit down and wait calmly. You look for the flashlight on your phone and shine it around the car to see if anyone else is there. There's no one. You're alone. You stand up and start to walk slowly through the train. You want to see if there's another human being on it, and also to reach the first car so you can talk to the driver and ask him when the subway will be running again, or to the conductor, if he hasn't already gotten off. You go from car to car and see nobody. When you reach the door to the driver's cabin, you knock on it, containing your rage. The door doesn't open. You keep knocking. You knock and yell until your fists start to hurt. "He left," you yell. "The son of a bitch left." You sit down and turn off your flashlight to save the battery. You're about to burst into tears, but you stop yourself. You feel that in the dark, one is truly alone.

You find you're struggling to breathe because of the heat when the doors open. This seems strange to you, since the electricity is still out, but you figure they probably open automatically, that it's related to safety. You get up slowly and stick your head out. Nothing, you can't see a thing. You call for help, but all you hear is the echo of your voice in the tunnel. You sit back down and consider your options. Either you stay where you are until the electricity comes back or you get off the train and walk along the tracks to the next station. It wouldn't be the first time a train had gotten stuck between stations and someone had to walk along the tracks. It's been on the news. But you have no guide, no light, no company. You wish the subway were bursting with people like it was yesterday morning, like it is every morning. You miss the immense, amorphous mass of strangers that is the human race. Again you feel like crying, but you shout, "Enough!" and make up your mind to solve the problem.

You turn on your phone's flashlight and sit down in the door frame. Slowly, you lower yourself to the ground. You walk carefully to the driver's cabin and shine the light through the window. The cabin is empty. "The goddamn son of a bitch," you say with hatred and irritation.

Which way? You don't really know where you are. In the middle of the solitary stations? It doesn't matter, you think, I have to find a station and pray it's not closed. Then you remember the train passed Congreso and that the next station is Pasco and understand you have to continue in the same direction. You decide to walk off to the side of the tracks, in case the electricity comes back on. You don't want to be electrocuted to death. It's hard for you to walk because of your heels, but you go slowly.

You're on your way when your phone turns off. "No!" you shout. You curse the day you bought this model, because the battery life is so short. In the dark, you feel something brush against your ankle. A rat. Or worse, something else, something you may never learn the nature of. You're disgusted. Why is this happening to me? you think. Your head feels full of fear, a frozen, hard fear. You start to cry slowly, helplessly, blindly. Alone. Without light you can't go on; without light you can't trust anything.

You breathe deeply, stand up straight, and calm yourself down. The goal is to find a station, that's it. You start walking very slowly with your hands out in front of you. You count your steps so you don't have to think about what's behind the darkness. Twenty, twenty-one. Fifty, eighty-four. You count out loud, to hear the echo of your voice so you don't feel so alone.

One hundred and fifteen. You feel a draft. "A station!" you yell. You take a few more steps and then your right foot can go no farther. You crouch down, feel around with your hands. "Stairs," you say euphorically. You start to climb them on all fours, when you feel someone take your hand. You can't see the hand helping you up, but you feel that it's rough and cold. "Thanks, I'm lost, the train stopped," you say. "Thanks." When you're standing in the station, you ask the stranger, who you can't see, where the exit is. The stranger doesn't respond. "Can you tell me where the exit is, please?" you repeat, worked up. Silence. With your hands out in front of you, you walk until you touch a wall. You keep touching walls. "Where's the piece-of-shit exit? It's all walls. Where's the fucking exit? Why won't you answer?" you yell, desperate. You need to find a door, a turnstile, anything. In the dark, you realize there's no exit, that everything is boarded up, that this is one of the stations that was closed down. You're going to have to go back to the tracks, so you keep walking, you need to get out of there. But when you turn around, you see two figures sitting on the edge of the platform, two men with their backs to you looking at the tracks. They're so white you can see them in the dark. They look like they're wearing boiler suits covered in dust, like they're workmen. They turn their heads, look at you, and open their mouths like there's a scream trapped inside them. You understand then that they are the ones waiting for you.

# ABOUT THE AUTHOR

**Agustina Bazterrica** is an Argentine novelist and short story writer. She is a central figure in the Buenos Aires literary scene. She won the prestigious Premio Clarín Novela for her second novel, *Tender Is the Flesh*, which has been translated into twenty-three languages. Several of the stories in *Nineteen Claws and a Black Bird* have also won awards, including First Prize in the 2004/2005 City of Buenos Aires Awards for Unpublished Stories and First Prize in the Edmundo Valadés Awards for the Latin American Short Story, among others.

## *Translator*

**Sarah Moses** is a writer and translator of French and Spanish. She has translated works by authors including Ariana Harwicz, Alberto Manguel, and Agustina Bazterrica, whose novel *Tender Is the Flesh* was also published by Scribner. Her story collection *Strange Waters* is forthcoming in 2024.